Westchester Public Library

Westchester, Illinois

HOURS

Monday - Friday	10:00 A.M. - 9:00 P.M.
Saturday	10:00 A.M. - 4:00 P.M.

The Indian brave on Dicky Boy

LOOKING FOR MIRACLES

A MEMOIR ABOUT LOVING

by

A. E. Hotchner

HARPER & ROW, PUBLISHERS

NEW YORK, EVANSTON,

SAN FRANCISCO, LONDON

FIRST EDITION

Designed by Janice Stern

Library of Congress Cataloging in Publication Data

Hotchner, A E
  Looking for miracles.
  Sequel to King of the hill. I. Title.
PZ4.H834Lo [PS3558.08]   813'.5'4   73–4091
ISBN 0–06–011965–9

This book is dedicated to my brother

Chapter 1

FAREWELL TO THE ICE WAGON,
BUT HELLO TO WHAT?

My job on the ice wagon was just about the best summer job in St. Louis. I'd stand there among the cold-steaming burlap-covered ice chunks sucking on ice chips while the wagon rumbled down the street with Mr. Manuche yelling "Eyeee-ees!" in a voice that rose up and into every kitchen. Little kids would run along behind the wagon begging for ice slivers or trying to get their mouths under the steady stream of ice-cold water that dribbled from the rear corners of the wagon.

When the wagon stopped for a sale, I'd pluck the ice pick from where it was stuck in the wagon's side, flip back the burlap, and pick-pick-pick in a straight line down the cloudy center of the ice block, splitting it neatly into the size Mr. Manuche wanted. Then I'd grab the tongs and dig its points into the sides of the ice chunk and push it forward onto the pad of burlap on Mr. Manuche's shoulder.

It was maybe 120 degrees out there in the St. Louis sun, with the street tar half melted, but I'd be standing there in the wet dark cave of the wagon, my Keds soaking in the icy water. At seven dollars a week it was a great summer job, all right.

I had worked for Mr. Manuche the summer before and I was supposed to start work for him again the day after I graduated from Soldan High School. The previous summer I had given my mother six of my seven weekly dollars, but this summer I was going to save it all because I was starting college in the fall, on a scholarship, and I needed every cent I earned to pay for my books and supplies.

One Saturday morning in May, I went over to see Mr. Manuche, but above the icehouse where it had said V. MANUCHE ICE & COAL, it now said SCHULTZ & SON. There was a boy my age out in front harnessing up Mr. Manuche's horse, Prince.

"Where's Mr. Manuche?" I asked.

"Gone," he said.

"Gone where?"

"Dunno."

"He sell his business?"

"Yup."

A big man with a lot of hair and tattoos came out of the icehouse onto the platform, pushing a hundred-pound block in front of him.

"Are you Mr. Schultz?" I asked.

"Yeah."

"I worked for Mr. Manuche last summer. I know the routes and I thought maybe you could use me."

"I got my son there."

"Well, could you use the two of us? I really know the routes and all the customers."

"You want to split your salary, John?" Mr. Schultz asked the boy.

"What salary?" the boy asked.

Mr. Schultz got a big laugh out of that. The boy spat on the ground and that made Mr. Schultz laugh all the harder, pointing his forefinger at him while he roared away.

I walked away feeling everything in my stomach. I had taken it for granted that I had this job, but now, without it, there was no way I could go to Washington University in the fall.

The first thing I felt was anger, which was usually the way I reacted when anyone got me in a corner. All right, I said to myself, I'll just go tell them to give their old scholarship to some rich kid who has money to buy books and supplies and pay for lab fees and all that. How could I possibly manage? My mother, who made a meager income from her Bell Company job, was behind in the rent and we skipped more meals than we ate. My father was still recuperating from his heart attack and couldn't have worked if he had had a steady job, which he hadn't.

After fast-walking a couple of blocks, I began to cool down. Anger left, feeling-sorry-for-myself moved in. I didn't want to go home for two reasons: one was that whenever anything like this happened, my brother, Sullivan, had a million questions to ask and I didn't feel like explaining everything to him; the other was that this was Saturday and I always stayed away on Saturday morning. We lived in three rooms above Sorkin's delicatessen, and directly across the roof from us was the Beth Israel Synagogue, where they prayed on Saturday. I really didn't mind the cantor's singing and all the congregation noises, but what used to drive me batty was this one old man who all morning long would keep coming out on the porch of the synagogue, directly opposite our windows, to have a coughing fit. He had twenty, thirty fits a morning and it was the kind of coughing that made his throat rattle. He would choke and turn redder and redder, each cough grinding deeper, gasping for air until finally when he was just about to suffocate he would hack up an enormous clinker, rasp it out of his throat, rear back and spit it out over the railing. You could hear it plop on the pavement below.

I thought about where else I could go and decided to see if Billy Tyzzer was home. Billy and I had been friends since grammar school when I taught him how to stop being a cunny-thumb and shoot marbles properly. Billy was rich and lived in a house with its own yard. He always had pretty good ideas about how to make money, like raising canaries. He had put me on to how to breed them, even lending me a female to mate with our bird, Skippy. It was a good marriage and they produced four babies that should have brought me five dollars apiece at the pet store, but when they were old enough to sell, the pet-store owner rejected them because they were all females. Canary females are worthless because they don't sing. But that certainly wasn't Billy's fault. His canaries produced babies at the same time as mine, six of them, and all six turned out to be males. Thirty dollars.

Billy was up in his room working on his stamp collection. He put down his magnifying glass and gave me the hand grip we had used ever since we had that secret club in the eighth grade.

"You know something?" he said. "I heard about a job only yesterday from a guy I used to go to camp with. There's this new camp that the CCC just built in the Ozarks and they're looking for counselors."

"Are you going to apply?"

"No. I'm going to work on my uncle's ranch in Texas."

"Well, do you think they'll take someone like me? I don't have a lot of experience."

"Just go over and see the director. I have his name. The YMHA is running the camp and they pay ten dollars a week. When I think of some of the finky counselors I've had . . . Just go on over."

4

I'd said I didn't have a lot of experience. I certainly didn't. If ever there was a city boy, I was it. Not only had I never been to camp, but I had never been out of St. Louis. Except for the time when my mother was in the Fee-Fee Sanitorium and I went to see her on the Creve Coeur trolley. I'd never been on a hike, couldn't swim a stroke, never been in a rowboat or canoe, never been on a horse, didn't know fauna from flora.

But this was a job—J-O-B—and maybe the only job that would come my way. None of the kids I knew had been able to find jobs; and the same went for most of their fathers. My father, after a long wait, had finally landed a PWA job but lost it five months later when he had his heart attack.

I phoned the camp director, Mr. Arnold Berman, who called himself "Chief." After all, it was Camp Hiawatha. He gave me an appointment for the following Thursday, which meant I had less than a week to become an experienced camp counselor.

What I did was to spend all the time I could at the public library. Sullivan would come along and read Tom Swift and the Rover Boys while I read every book on camping that they had on the shelves, plus the Boy Scout manual, cover to cover. Not only read, but memorized. At school I had developed a trick of being able to read a book just before an exam, remember the stuff practically word-for-word for the test, then let it evaporate right out of my head the following day. The Boy Scouts of America could have quizzed me about any merit badge (on paper) and they would have thought they were dealing with an Eagle Scout. Of course there's a world of difference between knowing how to start a fire without matches and being able to do it. But I figured there was little likelihood that Chief Berman would ask for any demonstrations in his office.

But I did practice what I could. Like at night I would step out our bedroom window onto the delicatessen roof; Sullivan would follow me. With the Boy Scout diagrams in my hand, I'd try to identify the constellations. Of course, I already knew the few easy ones, like the two Dippers, but I never could spot things like the Little Bear, the Dragon, the Whale, and the Peacock. Sullivan claimed he could see all of them.

"You don't see it? There it is—right there alongside the Big Dipper." He'd point his finger at the million stars up there and of course I had no way of knowing if he really saw what I couldn't see. My brother had a super-active imagination and it was hard to know with him what was make-believe and what was real. He had had some pretty awful years, so I guess when the reality got very bad, the make-believe came in handy.

What had made Sullivan's life so wretched was being farmed out so often. My father, like many others, had been unable to cope with the Depression, and as a result we became urban migrants, moving from one place in St. Louis to another, a jump ahead of the process servers. I went to eleven different grammar schools. We finally wound up in one room in the Avalon, a seedy hotel at Kingshighway and Delmar. My mother earned what she could at a variety of odd jobs, ranging from typing to selling lingerie to the ladies in the whorehouses in East St. Louis. But she could not work and also look after my young brother, who was then five. Her solution was to ship Sullivan to various relatives; he mostly boarded with my aunt and uncle in Keokuk, Iowa, who had several children of their own. Theoretically, my father was supposed to pay two dollars a week for Sullivan's keep, but he rarely had the two dollars to send. This resulted in a growing resentment against poor Sullivan, who was constantly berated for our father's dereliction by whoever was keeping him. Sometimes the irate relative would suddenly pack up Sullivan's meager belongings in his cardboard suitcase and send him back to us on the bus.

On those occasions when Sullivan did return to our family group, he lived in the practical fear that at any time he would again be farmed out. My father frequently discussed Sullivan's status in his presence as if he weren't there, a child-commodity to be shipped around like the watches my father used to sell before the Depression. I felt Sullivan's reactions, his hurts, very keenly, and as a result I developed a kind of subconscious guilt over being the Chosen One to stay with the family. But in all honesty, although I'd miss him when he was gone, I did benefit from his absence since I'd get a bigger portion of whatever food we managed to scrounge, and I'd have the bed all to myself. There were two beds in the room when we lived at the Avalon, with a screen in between. There was one full-sized double bed which my parents shared, and a smaller bed which I shared with Sullivan. We constantly quarreled over who was crowding who and I was forever drawing indented marks down the center of the sheet to delineate our respective territories.

Then, suddenly, he wasn't there to fight with any more, for no sooner did Sullivan get settled into school than my mother would find a job and off he'd go with promises that it wouldn't be for long. Sullivan was certainly aware that he was a burden both to those who kept him and to those who had sent him away. From five years of age on, Sullivan fully knew that, practically speaking, he was not wanted anywhere.

When he was away my mother yearned for him; occasionally she had hysterics, laughing and crying uncontrollably at dinner when his name was mentioned—but this faraway yearning was of no value to Sullivan. My mother tried to scrimp together enough extra money to telephone Sullivan once a week. Sometimes, though, she had to miss a week. One time, on the phone, she told him how much she missed him, and Sullivan, who was not a cryer, began to cry. "How can I hug you, Mama," he

7

asked, "when you're in the telephone?"

Sullivan finally came back for good, never to be farmed out again, when my mother got a regular job with the Western Union Company in May of 1936. The Western Union Company had a policy of not employing married women, but my mother had lied to get the job. I had just turned sixteen, and my brother was going on eleven. It was going to be our first summer under the same roof and I had promised to teach him to play tennis on the public courts in Forest Park.

But that's about the only way Sullivan figured in my summer plans. He had been away too long and too often for me to know much about him. Or, to be honest about it, to *care* much about him. We had very little in common. We didn't even look alike. I was predominantly freckles, wavy red hair, prominent nose. Except for a few dribbles on the tip of his nose, Sullivan was virtually unfreckled, straight dark hair, button nose. No resemblance. Nor in our personalities. I was aggressive, boisterous, verbal, tempestuous. Sullivan was placid, quiet, taciturn, introverted. He spent most of his time sitting in a chair in the front room reading adventure books about swashbuckling men in faraway places. Rafael Sabatini was his favorite author.

Curiously, the only times I had had a rise of brother feeling toward Sullivan was on those occasions when he had his bad earaches. Sullivan was susceptible to ear infections that caused excruciating pain and ultimately had to be relieved by an ear doctor who went inside his ear with a scalpel and lanced the infected area in order to drain the pus. The doctor gave no anesthetic for this and the pain was such that my mother and I had to hold Sullivan so the doctor could perform his surgery. My mother would hold Sullivan's legs and I would hold his head and arms, pinning his head against my chest, as the doctor maneuvered his forehead mirror for interior illumination. Sullivan would wail in anticipation of the knife's pain, and then scream and writhe as the scalpel pierced the infection. Once he bit my forearm rather severely. Holding him like that, as he suffered that barbaric pain, was when I came closest to feeling a sense of being his brother.

Sullivan had a strong attachment to me, a *dependence* on me, but not in a pushy way. For the most part, this dependence emerged as a strong identification with whatever I was doing; he virtually suffered as I suffered, shared my happinesses and triumphs, became depressed when I did, angry over the same things I got angry about, and the sports and hobbies (such as collecting cigar bands) that interested me interested him. So, naturally, he became all bound up in my seven-day crash program to become a camp counselor. He tried to read all the camp books after I read them, but he couldn't keep up with my voracious pace.

I also read a lot of Indian books. I figured that since they called it Camp Hiawatha and Berman called himself Chief, they would be bearing down pretty hard on the Injun motif. I memorized some Indian songs and tried to do the rain dance as described in one of the books. Sullivan said it looked more like the Big Apple. The day before the interview Sullivan gave me what he called an Indian Surprise Box. Inside it was a headdress he had made, using chicken feathers that had been plucked from Sorkin's chickens. Sullivan had spent a lot of time painting the feathers and sewing little beads on the headband. He suggested I wear it at the interview to impress Chief Berman.

I got to the interview a half hour early, but walked around the block a few times so it wouldn't look like I was too eager for the job. I could have spared myself the effort. Chief Berman's waiting room was packed with boys. My heart dropped. The woman at the desk gave me a number and I waited my turn. Most of the boys were eighteen or nineteen and you could tell just by looking at them that they could swim, hike, and paddle canoes. I kept going over the list of knots, trail signs, constellations, first-aid instructions, bird names, tree names, and all that, that I had in my pocket. But looking at the faces of the boys as they came out of Chief Berman's office, I was pretty sure that all the jobs would be filled by the time they got to me.

Chief Berman was stocky and muscular, with a thin straight mustache and hairy eyebrows. He was very well scrubbed and creased. He gave my fingernails a close look which made me glad I had remembered to scrape them with my pearl-handled penknife. I was pretty well scrubbed myself, but not creased. He asked me my age—I told him eighteen. He asked what experience I had had, and I said I had been a junior counselor and counselor at Camp Chickachuck in Oregon. (A name I picked out of the Camp Guide section of *Liberty* Magazine.) I also said I had spent a couple of summers at my uncle's ranch in New Mexico. (My uncle actually ran a men's-clothing store in Keokuk, Iowa.) Chief Berman asked me what my special interests were. I was thinking about the stream of boys who had been in before me, so I decided to lay it on thick. If the Chief had recently read the Boy Scout manual he might have found that my interests had a familiar ring to them, but as it was he listened intently as I ticked off my newfound knowledge of earth and sky.

Chief Berman looked at me intently. "Are you a leader?" he asked. He spoke in a stentorian voice with a lot of enunciation that made his pencil mustache bob around.

"How do you mean?" I asked.

"Are you a take-charge type?"

"Well, it might sound like bragging. . . ."

"That's all right—I like a man who can blow his own horn."

"Yes, sir. Well, I was captain of most everything I did. Baseball team, basketball, debate team, dramatic society, tennis team, president of the senior class . . ." (As a matter of fact, I *was* captain of the debate team.)

"I like secure men who know who they are and where they're going."

"Yes, sir." I was having a hard time keeping my eyes off his mustache.

"I've been a camp director for fifteen years and I've had good counselors and bad. I had this one counselor who got *homesick*, for God's sake, and one who was afraid of bugs. Why, I've even had a counselor who couldn't swim!"

"No!"

"Can you imagine anybody applying to be a counselor and they can't swim!"

"Unbelievable!"

"I kicked his bottom right out of there!"

"I should think so."

"Now, this camp is a real challenge. Brand new, carved out of the Ozark wilderness, a real challenge, wild animals, primitive, cut off from civilization . . ." He sprang out of his seat and whisked around the desk. "This is no sissy camp. I don't want any country-club counselors, get me? I want rugged men who can meet the challenge!" For emphasis he banged me on the arm with his fist.

I snapped up out of my seat. "It's my kind of camp, Chief!" I said. I almost saluted.

"Send in the next boy," he said, returning to his seat.

He was watching me, so I tried to walk out of there with a

tough swagger, but, skinny as I was, it probably only looked like I'd gone stiff in the joints.

My brother was waiting outside the Y. "How'd you do?" he asked.

"I don't know."

"He didn't hire you?"

"No. They let you know. There were a million guys being interviewed." I was feeling depressed. I'd laid it on too thick. I mean, captain of *everything* and all that.

"Boy, lemme tell you, they're loonies not to hire you. I seen those guys comin' out and they *couldn't* pass you up for creepers like that."

In my brother's eyes I was Tarzan, Jack Dempsey, and Franklin Roosevelt rolled into one. We walked along for a while, me worrying.

"What'll you do if you don't get the job?" Sullivan asked, joining my worry.

"Not go to college, I guess."

"You *gotta* go to college."

"Well, let's not talk about it."

"You gotta go," Sullivan said. "Listen, we won't let them do that to you!"

"Did you hear me?"

"And *Scaramouche.*"

"It's no wonder you're failing."

"I'm not failing. Looka there—a B, two Cs, and a D."

"That's as good as failing. There's never been a D in this house."

In the days that followed my interview for the counselor job, Sullivan worried as much about my not hearing from Chief Berman as I did. Convinced that I would be rejected, every day after school I tramped around looking for some other summer job, and Sullivan tagged along, but whatever I heard about or saw in the paper, there was always a line of grown men applying and I couldn't blame an owner for hiring a father instead of a boy of sixteen. The beauty of the counselor job was that it needed a boy, not a man. And ten dollars a week to be out in the open, playing games and having fun!

But as the days passed without word from Chief Berman, I got more and more discouraged. Sullivan tried to cheer me up with money-making suggestions: a wash-your-car-in-your-own-driveway service, a running-errands company, collecting bottles for the two-cent refunds—suggestions like that. I tried to get rid of Sullivan, because when I was miserable I liked to be alone, but there was no way to do it without seriously hurting his feelings.

Finally I heard from Chief Berman. It took me a while to get up enough courage to open the envelope. I had known from the start that I was going to be turned down. But I wasn't. Nor was I accepted. Would I please come in at my earliest convenience?

Sullivan sat on the steps of the Y and waited while I went in for my appointment. Chief Berman was on the telephone and motioned me to sit down. My hands were clammy. Sullivan and

I had been to the Varsity the night before and watched James Cagney as the jury filed in with the verdict. The way he suffered, wetting his lips, trying to swallow, his breath coming hard, that's how I suffered as I waited for Chief Berman to hang up the phone.

"Now, I have a problem with you," he said. "I was terribly impressed by your knowledge and camping know-how, but I don't think I can make you a regular counselor because you would simply be *too* knowledgeable for the head counselor of any group I put you into. It would undermine his authority with the other counselors, you see. On the other hand, you are really too young to be a head counselor—the other counselors would probably resent you."

My heart sank. Over-zealous salesmanship had done me in. "Oh, I don't know as much as I sound like I know," I said.

"You are very knowledgeable," Chief Berman said sternly.

"Yes, sir," I said, accepting the verdict.

"You have a positively brilliant grasp of astronomy."

"Yes, sir," I said, cursing the Boy Scout handbook.

"And Indian lore."

"Yes, sir."

"Do you think you can handle ten-year-olds?"

The lump that had been sinking in my throat suddenly halted. I blinked. "Do I think . . . Why, I have a brother who's ten years old. I have him and his friends around me all the time." Actually, Sullivan had no friends.

"Let me explain Camp Hiawatha to you. It's composed of four villages, each for a different age group. These four villages are self-contained except for eating—we have one main dining building. Now each of these villages is run by a chief counselor with a staff of two regular counselors and a junior counselor. I've been thinking of you for the ten-year-olds."

"Yes, sir." Lump in throat in the ascendancy.

"I have two counselors who are only eighteen, as you are, and a junior counselor who is seventeen, so it's possible, if you handle the situation correctly, that you could assert your authority as chief counselor."

Lump dropped in panic. "Chief . . . ?"

"It pays five dollars a week more. Now, what I want to know is, do you think you could handle it? This is a brand-new camp and there will be unusual problems—quite a challenge. What do you think?"

Fifteen dollars a week! For that amount of money I would have answered yes if he had asked me if I thought I could fly across the Pacific in *The Spirit of St. Louis.* "I enjoy leadership," I said.

"I warn you, it won't be easy. The campers are going to be a handful. Half of them will be coming from good homes and paying tuition. The other half will be here on scholarships—poor kids from tough neighborhoods. The haves against the have-nots."

"It doesn't bother me," I said. "I've been both."

When I emerged from the Y and saw Sullivan's worried face, I couldn't help bursting into loud laughter. The worry flew off his face and he did a little jig, running up and down the Y steps the way Bill Robinson did. "I knew it, I knew it, I knew it," he sang as he jigged up and down the steps.

"Me big chief counselor," I said, but suddenly I stopped exulting and felt very sad. I just stood there on the steps watching my happy brother. Happy over my good fortune. Happy that I was going to have a good summer and be able to go to college in the fall. Sullivan, who had never had a good summer in his life.

Until this moment I had never thought about *his* summer. I would be away at camp. My mother would be working every day at the telephone company, 8:30 to 5:30. And my father would make his daily abortive rounds of the downtown jewelry shops and department stores, trying to sell his watch straps. There was a firm in New York that sent him leather straps on consignment, and after each sale my father would pay them and take his small commission. But there weren't many sales since people who barely had money for bread certainly didn't have money for watches and watch straps. Also, the heart doctor had warned my father, after his miraculous recovery, that he had to take it very easy.

So standing there on the Y steps, I had one of those moments, rare for me, when I moved outside myself and realized what a grim summer was in store for Sullivan. In a way, looking at him that day, I was seeing him as I had not seen him before. His joyful dance had abated, but he was still smiling his big smile, two teeth missing.

"Look," I said, "I just thought of something. Wait here." I started back into the Y.

"Where you going?"

"Wait here."

I went back to Chief Berman's office and asked him whether my brother could qualify for one of the camp scholarships. He gave me an application blank.

"You won't favor him, will you?"

"He'll just be another camper to me," I said.

I didn't tell Sullivan what I had in mind. What he needed least in life was another disappointment. But whether he would be accepted at Camp Hiawatha or not, I had done something that startled me. In the past, I had always treated the members of my family as obstacles to be kept from my ambitious path. I asked for nothing, gave nothing. I lived under a family roof, but the atmosphere was contentious and the conditions depressing, so

20

I spent as much time *not* under the family roof as possible. School and after-school sports were my worlds. I was a star at school, heaped with praise and recognition. I had closer ties to certain teachers than I did to my family. But now, this unlikely moment with my brother, I had felt something inside me, really *felt* it. But in all honesty I would have to admit that rather than giving me a positive feeling, it simply disturbed me. Although I didn't admit it to myself, I was probably secretly anticipating that Sullivan's application, which I signed for him, would be rejected. I could feel good, then, over what I had tried to do for him, but not be saddled with the responsibility of having done it.

My main concern, however, in the days that followed my appointment as chief counselor of Indian Mound Village, was how in God's name I was going to maintain this hoax. I who had scarcely been out of St. Louis, never seen a camp, couldn't swim, couldn't canoe, couldn't ride—in fact, name any camp activity, I hadn't done it.

"And what if, in the meantime, Big Chief Berman contacts Camp Chickachuck and finds out I'm an impostor?" Sullivan and I were sitting on the grass at the Forest Park tennis courts, waiting for the period bell to sound.

"He won't."

"And what if he checks on me with Soldan High and discovers I'm only sixteen—just *turned* sixteen?"

"Why would he?"

"Because that's what people do—they check on you."

"I'll betcha he won't."

"He will. You just don't know."

"I'll betcha the agate shooter I won from Chris Donohue against your knife."

"And even if he doesn't check, what do you think he'll do

when we go into the water on the first day and I drown? . . . Oh, God, why did I ever get myself into this?"

"Stop worrying. You're gonna be super-colossal. You are at everything, aren't you?"

"I only do things I know I can do."

"Sure, but you can do everything."

"No I can't."

"Name me one thing you can't do."

"Swim."

"So, okay, you'll make yourself swim."

"I've tried. I can't."

"You mean that one time in the Mississippi?"

"I almost drowned. All I got out of that were leeches."

"One time don't count."

"Doesn't."

"Doesn't count. How about your telling me before the big game when you played McKinley for the championship that you couldn't hit curves?"

"I always flinched before the ball broke."

"You struck out the first three times, but the fourth time you socked a curve over the fence and won the game."

"Blind luck."

"Now me, I been trying all spring, but I still can't hit a curve."

"Hitting curves and swimming are different things."

"They know I strike out on curves, so that's all they throw me. I get scared and back away. They don't even choose me to play any more."

"I think it's because Mother's so afraid."

"Of curves?"

"I'm talking about swimming. What's curves got to do with this? She's so afraid of water."

"Did she ever go swimming with you?" I detected a slight edge of envy in his voice.

"Only one time. The Silvers had an outing at the Forest Park Highlands and we all went into the pool."

"You and Mom?"

"And the others. Mom stood in the two-foot wading section and held my hand and wouldn't let me splash around with the other kids."

"Why?"

"She said it was too dangerous for someone who didn't know how to swim."

"But how did she expect you to learn?"

"I don't know. But I was afraid of the water and didn't say a word in protest."

"I think I could learn to swim if I was around water."

"Did you ever try?"

"Once in Keokuk we all went down to the river, but there weren't enough tire tubes to go around and no one would share his with me. So I just sat on the bank and watched."

Chapter 3

IF YOU DON'T WANT TO GIVE UP
YOUR PEARL-HANDLED KNIFE, IT'S
BETTER TO LEAVE WELL ENOUGH ALONE

When I told Sullivan that he had been approved for a summer scholarship at Camp Hiawatha, he simply looked at me blankly; my words were so many darts that had not penetrated his protective armor. He had been sitting in the lopsided, sagged armchair in the front room, reading *Twenty Thousand Leagues Under the Sea* (I was trying to wean him away from Sabatini and onto Verne) when I came in with the letter of acceptance that had just come from the Y.

I had expected him to give a whoop and a holler, but, as I have pointed out, Sullivan was not conditioned for good news.

"Don't you get it?" I said. "You're going to be in my village! You're going to camp!"

"This summer? You mean—*now?*"

"That's right."

Sullivan looked worried. "I don't have anything for camp."

"Like what?"

"Like a knife."

"You don't need a knife."

"Oh, yes you do! A knife and a hatchet and a compass. But I'd settle for a knife."

"Believe me, you don't need all that."

"What if I got attacked by a bear or something?"

"There are no bears in the Ozarks."

"What are there?"

"Wildcats and snakes."

"I think I better not go."

"Now, Sullivan, you're being silly."

"All the other kids will have knives and hatchets. I know."

"How do you know?"

"I just know, that's all."

"But you've never been to camp in your life. . . ."

"Neither have you."

"What does that prove?"

"That you don't know any more'n I do. Those kids'll have canteens and hiking shoes and lariats. I've seen plenty a pictures."

"Sullivan, look, are you saying you don't want to go? After all the trouble I went to?"

"You shoulda asked me."

"But everybody likes going to camp!"

"Well, maybe I don't have any camp in my blood."

I took out my pearl-handled pocket knife. "Okay, here, now you've got a knife."

"But what'll *you* use?"

"Don't worry about me."

"You mean I can really have your pearl-handled knife?"

"For the summer."

He took the knife very carefully, handling it as if it were made of eggshells. "You know, I never had a knife."

"I know."

He opened the blade.

"Whatever you do, don't lose it," I said.

"Don't worry. It's my trusty old knife." He slashed at the air a few times. "Those snakes just better watch out."

I really didn't like lending him my knife. It had been given to me during that time at the Avalon Hotel by a friend of mine whom the cops had arrested for stealing. He had given it to me for a keepsake as the cops were taking him away. I never saw him again.

Sullivan would probably lose it. Served me right for having meddled with his summer. I needed the knife more than he did. Who ever heard of a chief counselor without a knife?

Chapter 4

ST. AARON AND HIS TRUSTY
HYDROPHOBIA SLAY THE WATER MOCCASIN

Camp Hiawatha was located in a primitive, rather impenetrable section of the Ozark lake region, which lies in central Missouri about two hundred miles west of St. Louis. The narrow, long, winding Lake of the Ozarks dominates the area, and Camp Hiawatha had been built on land that had been cleared on the southeast edge of the lake. It was a CCC project and I suspect the government chose this jungle-like site for the camp because clearing it gave a long stretch of employment to a large number of Civilian Conservation Corps workers. The only access to the camp was over a new, primitive dirt road that had been hacked out of the miles of dense forest and underbrush that intervened between the nearest highway and the camp. Just hacking the road must have provided jobs for half the unemployed of Missouri.

The counselors went to Hiawatha three days before the campers were to arrive. We went by bus from in front of the Y. The three days were to be used by Chief Berman to organize the camp and allow us to get acquainted. I was so nervous, so apprehensive I might somehow be exposed for the impostor I was, that I virtually didn't sleep the night before departure. Also, it was my first trip by myself out of St. Louis and I was over-excited about that. I sat in the back of the bus to make myself as inconspicuous as possible.

The trip took about seven hours, and the counselors horsed around and sang camp songs most of the way. Of course I didn't know any of the songs, but I was pretty good at moving my mouth and pretending to sing. Besides, no one was paying any attention to me in the back of the bus. Chief Berman was sitting next to the driver and every once in a while he told everyone to stay in their seats, but no one paid any attention to him. They sang things like "Drunk last night, drunk the night before, gonna get drunk tonight like I never got drunk before. . . ."

We stopped in Loose Creek to eat and use the toilet. While I was waiting my turn to get into the men's room, a short squat fellow with a heavy neck came over to me.

"I'm Mo Brennan," he said, putting out his hand. "I'm in your cabin." His hand was so thick I could hardly get a grip on it. He got in line with me.

"I'm really pissed off," he said. "I was supposed to be the wrestling and boxing counselor, but now Big Chief Pain-in-the-Ass tells me I'm switched to volley ball. Keeee-rist! Volleyball! Emphasis on team sport, he says. Volleyball! Listen, I'll run a team sport for him—the gang bang. I hear there's a Girl Scout camp across the lake."

The muscles in his neck appeared to ripple. His voice was a baritone growl, with the ends of sentences descending precipitously into his barrel chest. "Now, you're our cabin leader, right? So you go to the Big Chief and tell him ol' Mo Brennan is here for wrestling and boxing and not for fagging around with volleyball. Volleyball! You go tell him. He's over there having a doughnut."

"Well, why don't we wait till we get to camp?"

"What for?"

"I just think it's better."

"Crap. Go tell him now."

"No, I think it's best to discuss it at camp—now he's got his mind on other things."

"Then just tell him what I said and he better think about it. Go ahead, tell him that. I'd tell him myself, but I have a tendency to lose my temper."

I had moved up to next in line for the urinal. I realized that before I went in there to pee I had to make Mo Brennan understand that I was not going to be told what to do. Yet, I had no feeling of authority—just the opposite. My mouth was dry, and as Mo Brennan's voice got lower, mine got higher.

"Leave it to me, Brennan," I said, trying to force my voice down. I opened the door and went into the men's room. "I'll take care of it," I said as the door closed.

As I stood there, trying to pee, I felt frightened. We had not even reached camp and already I felt totally inadequate and fearful of the role I had taken on. Once we got to camp, how long would it take somebody like Mo to find out I didn't know my behind from a campfire?

The four villages of Camp Hiawatha were little camps unto themselves. My village, Indian Mound, was completely removed from the rest of the camp and could only be reached by a crude, narrow path that wound through dense woods. The village consisted of seven cabins made of logs and screen, a recreation hall of fieldstone and timber, a four-seater outhouse, a bank of showerheads (cold water only), and a central drinking

29

fountain and water dispenser. The cabins were designed for four occupants, which meant we would have twenty-four campers in Indian Mound, the seventh cabin to be shared by the four counselors.

In addition to Mo Brennan, my counselors were Paul Roth and Myron Barmowitz, who was the junior counselor—which meant he didn't get paid. Paul Roth was of the upper class. Paul Trimble Roth. I had seen pictures of Franklin Roosevelt as a teenager, and Paul Roth looked a lot like early Roosevelt. He was slightly obese and spoke with an Eastern prep-school accent. His clothes were very expensive but not new. Starting at age six, he had been going to the best summer camps in the country, but for the past two summers he had loafed around his family's estate in Ladue, which was the ritziest St. Louis suburb. His indolence, however, had irritated his father, who was a mover and a shaker, and this banishment to Camp Hiawatha had been devised as therapy. The terms of the banishment were that if Paul stuck it out for the summer, he would get a Marmon roadster on entering Yale in the fall. He smoked a lot and had a peculiar way of smiling at you that made you feel inferior. Mo Brennan and he loathed each other on sight.

Myron Barmowitz was skinny, hairy, and pimply. He had overlapped teeth and cracked his knuckles a lot. He was very quiet, rarely spoke, and had hiccups several times a day. He was interested in absolutely nothing but the horn he brought to camp, and he was passionate about that. It was a cornet that he kept in a state of high gleam. It nestled in a flannel bag inside its black leather case, and Corny, which of course was his immediate nickname, kept it under his pillow during the day and at the foot of his cot when he slept. He would sit on the edge of his cot by the hour, fingering the three valves while blowing silently into the cornet. But sometimes, especially during the

30

afternoon rest period, he would put the mute in and play it. He would lie on his cot, the golden horn pointed to the ceiling, his pimply cheeks puffed out, his eyes closed, playing slow and mournful jazz tunes.

I didn't mind Corny's music, but when Mo Brennan was in the cabin he raised hell. We finally worked out a compromise: when Mo was in the cabin, Corny would either not play the horn or else go play it in the rec hall. Paul Roth, nicknamed Bugs because of his deftness with a flyswatter, didn't care one way or another about Corny's playing, for he spent most of his free time playing chess with Babe Halpern, the assistant director (we called him Little Big Chief).

Two things happened the very first day of camp that miraculously gave me some standing among my fellow counselors and helped overcome my fear of being inadequate. The first incident occurred right at the start of the counselors' conference. Big Chief Berman displayed a large board on which a number of Indian relics had been mounted. "Now, the reason we are called Camp Hiawatha," he explained, "is that these arrowheads, spear tips, pottery pieces, and whatnot were found here during construction, proving that this region had once been an Indian settlement. That's our motif, our theme, our *raison d'être* —Indian!—and we must plan everything with that in mind. Yet, none of you knows beans about Indians. I want powwows and rain dances and braves on the warpath. Indian sing-a-longs, loincloths, headdresses, and totem poles. The works! Peace pipes. Tomahawks and teepees. War paint. Tracking in the woods without a compass. Now, fortunately there is one counselor among you who is steeped in Indian knowledge. I will ask him to meet with you every morning at nine A.M. and cover as much Indian stuff in three days as he can. I am putting him in charge of Indianizing Camp Hiawatha."

Then he called on me to stand up and be recognized. Which I did.

I should have been panicked by this unexpected and unwarranted assignment, but curiously I felt a surge of relief. Instead of having to perform some camp function that would reveal my ineptitude, I was being called upon to do something that no one there knew anything about. What's more, I had prudently brought the two library books *(All About Indians, The Indian Reader)* from which I had gleaned the information that had impressed Berman, and which I had anticipated using for my Indian Mound Village program.

In the afternoon of that first day, a second event occurred, even more unexpectedly, that helped give me an even better camp position. We were taken down to the lakefront to get acquainted with the water facilities. Before going, we were briefed by Bud Fischer, the nature counselor. He was a tall, lean, handsome man, twenty or so, who was a track star at the University of Missouri. He told us what we might expect in the way of animal life in the area, but emphasized that the only creatures that would give us any real trouble were two snakes, the copperhead and the water moccasin.

"They both abound in large quantities here," he said, "and they are both deadly. The copperheads are all around the camp in the underbrush, and the water moccasins are pretty heavy along the lakefront." He showed us large pictures of each snake. "We don't have any snake serum yet, so I urge you to be doubly cautious. Try to avoid brush and tall grass, which is the copperhead's hangout. He's not very large—usually under two feet—and he blends in with his surroundings—good camouflage, pale chestnut or hazel color with a lot of inverted Y-shaped dark blotches. His head has some red on it with cream streaks down the sides. What makes him so dangerous is that unlike the rattlesnake—and he is just as deadly—the copperhead strikes without movement or warning. And he's very aggressive.

"The water moccasin is just as deadly—in fact, they're cousins. He'll be in the vegetation right along the lakefront, or hanging on tree limbs that jut out over the water. He looks like just another twig. He hangs out there watching the water and when he sees something edible he drops on it, sinks in his fangs, swims around it till it dies, and then swallows it. If he's in the water he'll most likely be underside some floating object like a piece of wood. I think as long as the kids are swimming in our cleared beachfront area where the crib is, or away from the shores, they'll be all right. Otherwise exercise extreme caution. I hope to be able to trap a copperhead and a moccasin by the time the campers arrive so they'll have a firsthand look at the enemy. What makes the situation here so tough is that this is a new camp and the adjacent area has not yet reacted to the change. As far as these snakes are concerned, this is still their territory."

All the way down the trail to the lake, my ankles tingled with the expectation of being struck by a copperhead. But I was less concerned with the copperhead peril than I was with the possibility that we would all be expected to jump in and swim. Thankfully, that wasn't the case. What we did do was to get in several rowboats that were tied to the dock, six of us to a boat, and take a tour of the immediate lake. We rowed along in file (I sat in the stern of our boat with Paul Roth) and I felt rather exhilarated by this, my first boatride. The water was still and very clear and there were swarms of dragonflies that hovered and darted over the surface. Occasionally I could spot clusters of tiny fish wriggling near the surface. I breathed deeply, tasting air, filtered by the pines on shore, that St. Louis never knew.

At the end of the lake, where it curved, our file of rowboats turned and started back along the shore. Startled squirrels and rabbits broke for cover. I spotted a chipmunk (I didn't know it was a chipmunk until Paul identified it) sitting on a rock. Two big hawks appeared over the trees, soaring side by side, their wing tips almost touching, and as we were all looking up at them—that's when the snake dropped into the boat.

It fell with a thud at the feet of the two counselors who were rowing. They immediately dropped their oars and scuttled backward over their seat. The snake started to wriggle along the bottom of the boat. There was no doubt it was the water moccasin we had seen in Bud Fischer's photograph. The two counselors in the bow of the boat jumped overboard. They were immediately followed by the two counselors who had been rowing.

"Come on," Paul said, tugging on my arm, "let's go." He dived over the side. I sat there caught in the transfixes of my fear of the water and my fear of the snake. The counselors in the water were yelling at me to jump. The snake had stopped and raised his head to reconnoiter. I felt light-headed and weak. I didn't move, just sat there with my eyes fixed on the snake. The only desperate thought I had was that perhaps I could let myself over the side and hold on to the boat. But I realized that that would leave my hands vulnerable to the moccasin. And besides, what if I slipped? I was too terrified of the water even to try that. My mother was there in the boat with me—warning me, exhorting me about the water. I was terrified of the snake, but it was less menacing than the water. There was that time I had put my head in the water and water went up my nose. Suffocating, coughing, gasping—that was how it was to drown.

The snake suddenly lowered his head and began to move toward me. I could feel a rush of adrenalin. I grabbed one of the paddles and sprang up. I began shouting at the snake as I

34

smashed at him with the paddle. Just a gibberish of words, angry words, as I tried to kill the snake. I missed him. The blade of the oar was too wide to be maneuverable. I grazed his tail and spun him onto his back, but he immediately righted and kept coming. The counselors were screaming for me to jump. One of the other rowboats was hurrying alongside. I reversed the oar, holding it now by the blade. The water moccasin had cleared the seat. I came down on him with all my might and crushed his head. If I had missed him I probably would not have had time for another shot at him. I pounded him again and again and again with the oar, squishing his insides all over the bottom of the boat. I was mad as hell. It was fear, of course, but it looked like anger. Two of the boats finally came alongside and I stopped. I sat down on the stern seat, breathless and exhausted. My hands began to shake. Big Chief Berman and Little Big Chief Halpern, who had been in the lead boat, stepped onto my boat. They looked at the dead, battered water moccasin. Chief Berman picked it up by the tail and held it up for everyone to see. They all applauded and cheered and whistled. Little Big Chief Halpern clapped me on the back.

Fear had made me a hero.

Chapter 5

THE TWO-HANDED BROOM SWAT AS
ADMINISTERED ON THE SEAT OF
REASON BY THE ENLIGHTENED LEADER

My brother arrived on the first bus of campers, with all of his belongings in an old knapsack that my father had saved from the World War. My father had never actually been in uniform, but they had already issued some equipment to him at the induction center when his deferment came through.

Sullivan spotted me as he entered Indian Mound with his group, and the apprehension on his face changed into a self-conscious smile. We walked toward each other and suddenly he thrust out his hand and we shook hands. It occurred to me that we had never shaken hands before.

There were three categories of campers: (1) kids whose parents could afford to pay the sixty-dollar fee; (2) kids who came from "good homes" but who could not afford to pay because their fathers were unemployed; (3) kids who came from tough, slum homes, whose families had suffered about as much before the Depression as they did during it. It was this third group that caused the trouble in the beginning.

Only a few of the campers knew each other before coming to camp, but in a very short time groups were instinctively identified and formed. A big, swarthy boy with a husky voice, nicknamed Horse Face, assumed command of the tough group three. By the second day he had established a hold over all twenty-four boys. He and his pal, Knuckles, a skinny, ratty boy with a broken front tooth, went on a tour of all six cabins to inspect what each camper had brought to camp. Horse Face helped himself to whatever he saw that he wanted. The few who put up protests were immediately silenced by having their arms jammed up behind them to their shoulder blades.

On the third day of camp, the peace and quiet of the afternoon rest period were suddenly pierced by a fierce commotion in one of the cabins. The intensity of the sound sent Mo Brennan and me on the run.

The ruckus was coming from my brother's cabin. There were seven or eight boys in there, several of whom were shouting at Horse Face, who, when we arrived, was circling a table in the center of the room with a rusty bayonet in his hand. Circling with him, trying to keep the table between them, was my brother, Sullivan, who was half his size.

Horse Face was shouting, "Give it to me or I'll stick you!" As I started into the cabin, Horse Face made a leap over the table to grab Sullivan, who made a simultaneous dive under the table to avoid Horse Face's leap.

Mo and I grabbed Horse Face, who yelled, "Let hold of me, you finks!" I had to bend his hand into his wrist to get him to drop the bayonet.

"What the hell's going on?" Mo growled.

"Gimme my shiv!" Horse Face yelled. "It's my property!"

"Why was he after you?" I asked Sullivan.

Sullivan didn't answer, but opened his hand and revealed the

37

pearl-handled pocket knife that I had given him.

"Whose knife is that?" Mo demanded.

"It's mine," Sullivan said.

"He tried to take it off him," one of the boys in the cabin said, "the same way he took my key chain."

Mo grabbed Horse Face by the arm. "Who the hell do you think you are?"

"I'm a damn side more'n you are," Horse Face said.

I could see Mo's neck muscles thicken and rise, and I was afraid he was going to slug Horse Face, who stood around five feet and weighed maybe ninety vicious pounds. "All right, all of you get back to your own cabins," I said. "You, too," I said to Horse Face, pushing him out the door in front of us. We followed him back to his cabin. He stopped a couple of times and Mo gave him a shove in the back to get him going.

"You've got to let him know who's boss," Mo said to me in a voice Horse Face couldn't hear. "These kids'll run us ragged if you don't."

"What do you suggest?"

"Beat his ass off."

"Well, first I think I'll give him a good talking to."

"*Him?* Hell, talking is working on the wrong end of him. Beat his ass off, I tell you."

"If talking doesn't work, I'll report him to Berman."

"You're going to *what?* What kind of camps did you work at? You're the head counselor, aren't you? Christ, you go snitching to Berman and these kids'll be rooting for Horse Face."

"Maybe you're right. You see, I'll tell you, Mo, I've never been a head counselor before."

"You goddam well *run* this place. You're Mr. Big. These kids are chicken poop and they better believe it."

Horse Face kept his belongings in a thoroughly battered foot-locker.

"Open it up," I said.

"Up yours," he said.

Mo gave me a look.

"You heard what I said."

"That's my private property!" Horse Face shouted. "You got no rights to look into it." He plopped himself on top of the footlocker.

"Get up," I said.

"Up yours," he said.

"I said, get up."

"And I said up yours. And up your baby brother's."

Mo Brennan put both his hands around Horse Face's neck and lifted him off the trunk, choking him some in the process.

"God damn you, you wait'll I tell my father!" Horse Face shouted in his raspy voice. An instant picture of his father flashed across my eyes.

Mo held Horse Face by the hair at the back of his head while I opened the footlocker. There were a few items of clothing, rumpled and soiled; all the rest were articles of war. Clubs, knives of every description, slingshots, two hatchets, a BB gun, lengths of chain, homemade spears, rusty handcuffs, boards with nails in them—an awesome arsenal.

"What's all this for?" I asked him.

"Protection, that's what."

"Yeah? And who's supposed to protect us against you?" Mo asked.

"Keep your dirty hands off my stuff."

I began to feel my anger rising. Horse Face's three cabin mates were sizing me up. So was Mo Brennan. This little gangster had to be put in his place if I was to run Indian Mound. My temper had risen to a boil. I grabbed a broom that was standing next to the door.

"Bring him outside," I said to Mo. Mo marched Horse Face through the door and into the clearing in front of the adjoining cabins. There would be a good audience.

"Bend over," I said to Horse Face.

"Up yours," he said.

Mo grabbed him by the hair, yanked his head down, and held him that way. I drew back the broom and began slamming Horse Face across the behind. It was a heavy broom and I was able to get a resounding thud out of it. Horse Face yelped, but Mo held him firm as I laid into him with that broom. Pieces of straw flew off it as I put my whole weight behind every wallop.

When I let up, Mo yanked Horse Face's hair up, straightening him up. Horse Face was half crying.

"You, you—you'll get it when I tell my old man!"

"You stay in line, Horse Face," I said, "and no more backtalk or I'll wear out every broom in camp on you."

"Yeah? You and who else?"

"All right!" I said, grabbing the broom. "Ten more!"

Mo grabbed his hair.

"No! No!" Horse Face shouted. "I didn't mean it. Honest!"

"Then apologize."

Mo released his hair.

"I said apologize."

"For what?"

"For that backtalk."

"What backtalk?"

"Ten more!"

"Okay! All right! I apologize. That suit you?"

We took Horse Face's trunk over to the rec hall and locked

it up. At first I felt there was something Dickensian about what had happened, with me on the side of the *Oliver Twist* heavies. But then I recalled the birch-whipping headmaster in *Tom Brown's School Days* and felt better about it. Mo had taught me my first lesson as head counselor. In tough cases like this, one must deal with the seat of reason. But I would have felt better if I had been able to deal with Horse Face without the broom.

Chapter 6

BETTER TO LOSE YOUR MONEY
AND YOUR FRIENDS, THAN TO LOSE
YOUR CENTER OF GRAVITY

To my dismay, Sullivan was not having a good time. He was the youngest and smallest boy in his cabin, and the activities of camp were even stranger to him than they were to me. I tried to spend a little time with him every day during the afternoon rest period. The rest period was not intended as rest, like bed rest; it was simply a quiet hour when the camper was on his own. Sullivan and I often took a walk down to the lake and back.

"If I just had a friend," Sullivan said, "it would be lots better. But every time I think I have one, somebody steals him."

"You'll find one."

"Maybe not. I never had a friend in Keokuk."

"Perhaps you didn't try. You didn't like Keokuk, remember, and you didn't know how long you'd be there."

"Oh, I *tried.* There was this one boy named Virgil, I came right out and asked him to be my friend, but he said he couldn't."

"Did you ask him why?"

"Uh-huh. He said because he hated me."

"He *hated* you? He said that? What had you done to him?"

"Nothing, I tell you. I actually thought he was my friend. That's the trouble with me—people I scarcely know hate me."

"Now, come on, Sullivan, that's silly."

"Then how come I haven't got a friend? Answer me that. The three guys in my cabin pal around together, but not with me. You know, like when they go up for meals, they tell me to go walk with someone else."

"Would you like to switch to another cabin?"

"No, it'd be the same thing. I guess I just don't have any palship in me. But I sure wish I did. I bet I could be pretty good at it if I had the chance."

I tried to say things to reassure him that he had as much palship in him as anyone else, but his realistic appraisal of past events was stronger than my assessment of his potential.

"Look, if I had palship in me, I'd have a friend, wouldn't I?"

I didn't really have an answer for that.

There was one camp event that Sullivan did get excited about. If a camper had a birthday that occurred while camp was in session, the event was celebrated in the dining hall with a candled cake, a chorus of "Happy Birthday," and a gift from Big Chief Berman. The gift was invariably some useless object like a Boy Scout calendar, but Sullivan was looking toward his birthday with great anticipation. I don't want to sound maudlin, but the simple fact was that Sullivan had never had a birthday celebration. Nor had I. Our family was so poor that eating and paying the rent was a constant, all-consuming struggle, and there simply was no time, no money, no atmosphere for birthdays, Christmases, Thanksgivings, or anything else. Sullivan had never had a birthday party, a birthday cake, a birthday present. I kept a five-year diary and every birthday and every Christmas, one entry on top of the other, there was a mournful notation to the effect that my birthday had not even been mentioned, and that Christmas had passed with no tree, no presents, no stockings hung. In a way it was better to treat these occasions as non-events, for if you have no way to celebrate something that calls for food and presents, it is perhaps better to ignore it altogether.

Not only had Sullivan never had a birthday party of his own, he had never been invited to one. Sullivan would say that this was because he didn't have a friend, but more likely it was because we moved around so much we were never anywhere long enough for him to get on anyone's list.

As for his imminent Camp Hiawatha birthday, what Sullivan mostly talked about was the cake. He knew I had made friends with Floyd, the cook, and he asked me to have him write on the cake: A MILLION HAPPY BIRTHDAYS. I said I would.

Floyd was a tall, bony man with a sunken chest who had hair coming out of his nose and ears. He wore a white undershirt, white duck pants, and a white overseas-type cap that he kept cocked over one ear. His bottom teeth, from eyetooth to eyetooth, were missing. He had a heart tattooed on one arm that read, OH, ALICE! and a long wriggling snake on the other that ran from his shoulder to his elbow. He always had a cigarette hanging out of his mouth. He talked a lot and constantly sipped from a mug that had TEA written on it. I made it a point to spend a lot of time in the kitchen talking to him. After all our lean years, and all the meals we skipped for want of something to put on the table, just to look at all that food and watch Floyd work on it and smell it cooking was a great pleasure.

Besides, I loved to listen to Floyd, who told me about his life and travels and all the wonderful practical jokes he had played on people. Floyd loved practical jokes. He even pulled a few in camp. The best was the one he pulled on Big Chief Berman.

Somehow Floyd got hold of a piece of stationery from the Girl Scout camp across the lake. He snuck into the camp office and typed out a letter on the Girl Scout stationery addressed to Big Chief Berman saying as how Miss Rosemary McMartin, who was the good-looking director of the Girl Scout camp, would like to come to see him for dinner on such-and-such a date to discuss the possibility of mutual activities. Floyd signed it Rosemary McMartin and put it in Berman's letter box.

The Big Chief got all excited when he read the letter, and came into the kitchen and told Floyd to cook a really special dinner and have it served in Berman's cabin. The evening Miss McMartin was supposed to arrive, the Chief had his cabin all fixed up with flowers and candles on the table. He finally telephoned across the lake, around nine o'clock. Miss McMartin said that she didn't know what he was talking about and, besides, the last thing she wanted was to mingle her girls with our boys. Floyd had let me in on the joke; I met him in the kitchen after lights out. He got me laughing so hard I almost choked as he and I ate up the special dinner he had fixed for Big Chief Berman and his lady visitor.

The only thing I didn't like about Floyd was how he was always complaining about his wife. My mother and father were at each other so much that I could do without any more man-woman beefs. Floyd didn't spend much time with his wife, since he always had cooking jobs on boats or at camps, but every time he got a letter from her he was full of complaints. "Another thing," he'd say to me, "this wife of mine has got a thing about bills. It's only the twenty-fifth of the month, I already got this letter giving me hell cause I ain't sent her money to pay the bills which she is going to receive—get that, *going to receive*—on the first of the month. You ever hear of anything like that? These times, if you get paid at all it's a miracle, she's having a heart attack because she can't pay out the bills twenty minutes after she gets 'em. It's the thirtieth of the month, she's already running up to the landlord's apartment. Hello, Mr. Grevenrood, I got your rent for you. I got patches in my pants, she pays off the furniture four months early. If she can't go to the electric company's office on the day she gets their bill, she starts crying. It's a very emotional thing with her. Ah, well, she was an orphan, and I guess she's afraid."

Horse Face went after my brother again. Not about the pocket knife, about something else that was never explained to me. He had it in for Sullivan, I suppose, because Sullivan was a way to get at me. When I remonstrated with him, it was the same feisty, hard-mouthed Horse Face, so we had to have another shellacking with the broom. In his rage, Horse Face called me a freckled fruit, and called Mo, Gorilla Ass. There was a cookout that night with hot dogs and marshmallows, so in addition to fifteen broom swats I banished Horse Face to his cabin. Deprivation of the hot dogs and marshmallows seemed to hurt him more than my wallops. I instructed Corny to find a heavier broom.

I'd thought I could handle Mo's gripe about volleyball by ignoring it, but Mo was not one to be ignored. "You go up and tell Big Chief Pain-in-the-Ass," he said, "or I do. Which is it?"
    "Volleyball's not so bad, Mo—why don't you give it a try?"
    "I gave it a try. In the sixth grade. Well?"
    "Okay."
    "You've said that before. Every time I mention it you say okay, but you don't do anything."

"Okay."

"Okay when?"

"Leave it to me."

I didn't talk to Berman, but to Little Big Chief, Babe Halpern. Babe was a senior at Mizzou who had played guard on the varsity football team until he tore up his knee. He was a tall, beefy fellow who was always cheerful—in fact, jovial. He had a full laugh that came from his belly and he got along with everyone. I envied him his personality. I even tried to imitate him, but I didn't have that kind of laugh. Also I just wasn't the type to get along with everybody. Mo Brennan told me he had been at the football game when Babe had been hurt and that Babe was holding his knee in agony and weeping as they carried him off the field. I couldn't imagine Babe shedding tears. He stood six three or four and weighed around 220. When he talked to someone he had a habit of putting his arm around him and leaning down to lessen the distance between them. Mo said that Babe was Phi Beta Kappa in psychology; you could tell that psychology was his dish from the way he handled problems. Like Mo's.

"You tell Mo I think he's absolutely correct about the wrestling. That's his specialty and that's why he was brought here. Tell him I'll arrange with Chief Berman that Mo will have both —volleyball in the morning and wrestling in the afternoon."

Mo grumbled about the compromise, but the next morning he strung up a volleyball net and held his first session. He sat on a stool beside the net and limited his participation to adjudicating squabbles, but when his wrestlers assembled in the afternoon he got right onto the mat with them to demonstrate the various holds and techniques.

To my surprise, Sullivan enrolled with the flyweight wrestlers. It was the first activity he had shown any interest in. I asked Mo to give him a little special attention.

"I already have," Mo said. "I was impressed with his equilibrium. First-rate center of gravity. Hard to pull off his feet. He'll be all right if he can take it. Can he take it?"

"I should think so," I said.

Chapter 7

CORNY IN THE PIT AND MO ON THE
PENDULUM AND ALL THE RATS ON ME

In the eyes of the Indian Mound campers, I never really became head counselor until the night of the "Pit and the Pendulum" bonfire. I had no idea it would have the effect on the boys that it did.

What I had planned was for the campers to sit around a nighttime bonfire while I recited and acted out an abridged version of a short story by Edgar Allan Poe called "The Pit and the Pendulum." I had selected a site in a clearing back of the rec hall. There was a slope there that ran down to a flat grassy place which is where we planned to build the fire. At the fringe of this grassy flat was a large sycamore tree whose heavy branches hung above the flat. The afternoon of the bonfire I sent Corny to dig a square four-foot hole beneath the branches.

It was good and dark when we led the campers by flashlight down to the bonfire. We seated them in a tight circle around the fire, which cast dancing colors and shadows on the surrounding slope. The fact that we were situated at the bottom of this slope, encased by it, markedly contributed to the atmosphere of the story I was about to tell them. When they first sat down, the boys were noisy and full of wisecracks, the loudest voice, of course, belonging to Horse Face, but my first line quickly shut them off:

"The sentence—the dread sentence of death—was the last of distinct accentuation which reached my ears. I saw the lips of the black-robed judges, but then the figures of the judges vanished, as if magically, from before me; the tall candles sank into nothingness; their flames went out utterly; the blackness of darkness supervened; all sensations appeared swallowed up in a mad rushing descent as of the soul into Hades. Then silence, and stillness, and night were the universe. I had swooned."

I fell to the ground, stretched out lifeless beside the bonfire for a full minute. There wasn't a sound from the campers. Then I stirred and continued my recitation from my supine position.

"When I recovered, I lay upon my back, unbound. I reached out my hand, and it fell heavily upon something damp and hard. I quickly opened my eyes. The blackness of eternal night encompassed me. I struggled for breath. The intensity of the darkness seemed to oppress and stifle me. I at once started to my feet . . ."

I carefully rose from the ground and proceeded to act out the story as I told it.

". . . trembling convulsively in every fiber. I thrust my arms wildly above and around me in all directions. I felt nothing, yet dreaded to move a step, lest I should be impeded by the walls of a tomb. Perspiration burst from every pore, and stood in cold big beads upon my forehead. I cautiously moved forward, with my arms extended, and my eyes straining from their sockets in the hope of catching some faint ray of light. My outstretched hands at length encountered some solid obstruction. It was a

50

wall, seemingly of stone masonry—very smooth, slimy, and cold. I started to make a circuit of the walls, but I had not counted on the extent of the dungeon or upon my own weakness. The ground was moist and slippery. I staggered onward for some time, when I stumbled and fell. Sleep soon overtook me as I lay."

Before I lapsed into sleep, I crooked up my head and looked around me at the faces of the campers: they were white, intense, eyes wide, nails chewed, knuckles bit. As I had discovered in my Soldan histrionics, a good audience inspires an actor's performance, and that's what was happening here. "When I awoke, I cautiously walked across the slimy stone floor of my cell, tripped, fell, discovered that my head was suspended out over a very deep, water-bottomed pit that occupied the center of the dungeon." There was a distinct murmur from my audience when they saw my head hung over the edge of Corny's pit. "Shaking in every limb, I groped my way back to the wall, where again, after a stretch of agony, I fell asleep.

"When I awoke, the dungeon was awash with light. The walls, which I had taken for masonry, I could now see were made of huge plates of iron jointed together. I now lay upon my back, and at full length, on a species of low framework of wood. To this I was securely bound by a long strap that passed in many convolutions about my limbs and body, leaving at liberty only my head, and my left arm to such extent that I could, by dint of much exertion, supply myself with food from an earthen dish which lay by my side on the floor."

I strained to get my left hand a few feet away from my body, and I let out an animal groan that elicited a nervous response from my audience. "Looking upward, I surveyed the ceiling of my prison. It was some thirty or forty feet overhead, and constructed much as the side walls. On one of these ceiling panels

51

was the painted figure of Time as he is commonly represented, save that, in lieu of a scythe, he held what, at a casual glance, I supposed to be the pictured image of a huge pendulum, such as we see on antique clocks. It was situated directly above me, but as I gazed at it I realized that it was not a painting at all but that the pendulum was in motion. Its sweep was brief, and of course slow."

At this moment there appeared, from just below a bough of the sycamore tree, a gleaming, sharp-edged blade that slowly began to swing from side to side. This elicited a chorus of sucked breaths from the campers.

"A slight noise attracted my notice, and, looking to the floor, I saw several enormous rats traversing it. They had issued from the well which lay just within view to my right. Even then, while I gazed, they came up in troops, hurriedly, with ravenous eyes, allured by the scent of the meat. It required much effort and attention to scare them away."

Several rat-like forms came hurtling out of the pit, moving about rapidly, in and out of the pit. The boys recoiled and shrieked and clung to one another. In the semi-darkness, the stuffed socks that Corny was pitching out of the pit and pulling back with erratic jerks by their strings could just as well have been sharp-fanged rats. Above me, Mo Brennan, completely hidden by the sycamore's foliage, was slowly lowering the sweeping pendulum, which was the grounds keeper's sickle attached to a broom handle.

"After a while I took my eyes off the rats and cast my eyes upward. What I then saw confounded and amazed me. The sweep of the pendulum had increased by nearly a yard, its velocity was much greater, and it had perceptibly descended. I now observed—with what horror it is needless to say—that its nether extremity was formed of a crescent of glittering steel, about a foot in length, the under edge as keen as that of a razor; it hissed as it swung through the air.

"I could no longer doubt the doom prepared for me by monkish ingenuity in torture. Having failed to plunge into their pit by the merest of accidents, they had now devised a different destruction for me. Inch by inch, down, down it came until it swept so closely over me as to fan me with its acrid breath. The odor of the sharp steel forced itself into my nostrils. I prayed—I wearied heaven with my prayer for its more speedy descent. I grew frantically mad, and struggled to force myself upward against the sweep of the fearful scimitar. And then I fell suddenly calm, and lay smiling at the glittering death, as a child at some rare bauble."

Mo had lowered the sickle to about an inch above my body and I began to get concerned that, from above, he might not have an accurate perspective on just how close to me he was penduluming that blade. Corny kept the rats darting in and out of the pit and I could tell from the surrounding sounds that the boys were as concerned about that sickle blade as I was.

"Even amid the agonies of that period, the human nature craved food. With painful effort I outstretched my left arm as far as my bonds permitted, and took possession of the small remnant which had been spared me by the rats. As I put a portion of it within my lips, there rushed to my mind a half-formed thought of joy—of hope. Down—steadily down crept the blade. To the right—to the left—far and wide—with the shriek of a damned spirit! to my heart, with the stealthy pace of the tiger! I alternately laughed and howled. Down—certainly, relentlessly down! It vibrated within an inch of my bosom! I struggled violently—furiously—to free my left arm. Down—still unceasingly—still inevitably down! I gasped and struggled at each vibration. I shrunk convulsively at its every sweep.

"It was *hope* that prompted my nerves to quiver—the frame to shrink. It was *hope*—the hope that triumphs on the rack—that whispers to the death-condemned even in the dungeons of the Inquisition. I saw that some ten or twelve sweeps would bring the steel in actual contact with my robe—and with this observation there suddenly came over my spirit all the keen, collected calmness of despair. For the first time during many hours—or perhaps days—I *thought*. I proceeded at once, with the nervous energy of despair, to attempt the execution of my thought, and my thought had turned to the rats—wild, bold, ravenous, their red eyes glaring upon me as if they waited but for motionlessness on my part to make me their prey. I had been waving my free hand above the dish to keep them from devouring the last of its contents. In their voracity, the vermin frequently fastened their sharp fangs in my fingers. With the particles of the oily and spicy viand which now remained, I thoroughly rubbed my binding wherever I could reach it. Then I lay breathlessly still.

"One or two of the boldest rats leaped upon me and smelled at the binding."

Corny tossed a couple of socks right on me to the horror of my listeners.

"This seemed the signal for a general rush of the ravenous animals from the pit and they swarmed all over me."

Corny fired a salvo of rats upon me from the pit. Mo was now grazing my shirt with the blade of the sickle.

"The measured strokes of the pendulum disturbed them not at all. They pressed—they swarmed upon me; they writhed upon my throat; their cold lips sought my own as they busied themselves with the anointed binding. Disgust, for which the world has no name, swelled my bosom and chilled my heart. Yet one minute, and I felt that they would chew through the binding. It loosened. I lay still. I was *free.* The binding hung in ribands from my body. But the stroke of the pendulum already pressed upon my bosom. It had divided the serge of my robe. Twice again it swung, and a sharp sense of pain shot through every nerve. But the moment of escape had arrived. At a wave of my hand my deliverers hurried tumultuously away. With a steady movement—cautious, sidelong, shrinking, and slow—I slid from the embrace of the binding and beyond the reach of the scimitar. *I was free."*

There was a great sigh of relief and a cheer from the boys as the rats all scurried back into the pit and the pendulum disappeared quickly into the sycamore tree. But the cheer had not even died away when I plunged into the penultimate peril.

"But wait! There came to my nostrils the breath of the vapor of heated iron! A suffocating odor pervaded the prison! I panted! I gasped for breath! There could be no doubt of the design of my tormenters—oh! most unrelenting! oh! most demoniac of men! I shrank from the glowing metal of the walls as they started to move toward the center of the cell. . . ."

There now advanced toward me a wall of fire, forcing me backward, as Paul Roth, hidden behind the tree, began to push the fiery wall in my direction. The pushing device was a rake affixed to the base of the wall. The wall was a six-foot square of limbs covered with rags that had been soaked in kerosene. The flaming rags gave off an intense heat and an acrid black smoke that pervaded the area.

"Amid the thought of the fiery destruction that impended, the idea of the coolness of the well came over my soul like balm. I rushed to its deadly brink. I buried my face in my hands—weeping bitterly. The heat rapidly increased, and once again I looked up. The cell had been square, but in an instant it had shifted its form into that of a lozenge as the fiery walls moved toward each other, destined to force me into the pit. I could have clasped the red walls to my bosom as a garment of eternal peace. 'Death,' I said, 'any death but that of the pit!' And now flatter and flatter grew the lozenge. . . .'"

Paul had moved the burning wall so close to me I could feel my skin getting parched.

"'I shrank back—but the closing walls pressed me resistlessly onward. At length for my seared and writhing body there was no longer an inch of foothold on the floor of the prison. I struggled no more, but the agony of my soul found vent in one loud, long, and final scream of despair. . . .'"

I let loose with a scream that probably startled my mother in St. Louis.

"'I felt that I tottered upon the brink—I averted my eyes. . . .'"

I was indeed tottering on the brink of Corny's pit, the fire just about igniting me as Mo Brennan dropped out of the tree and landed beside the pit.

"'There was a loud blast as of many trumpets! The fiery walls rushed back! An outstretched arm caught my own as I fell, fainting, into the abyss. It was that of General Lasalle. The French army had entered Toledo. The Inquisition was in the hands of its enemies.'"

I collapsed into Mo's arms as Paul quickly withdrew the fire wall. Corny and Paul then helped Mo lift my unconscious form and the three of them in solemn procession carried me back to the cabin as the boys huddled behind them for the walk back to their cabins in the dark.

It was a hard and fast camp rule that all lights had to be out by ten o'clock, but that night in Indian Mound Village *no* lights went out. All through the night there was a steady stream of boys coming to the counselors' cabin. Some reported strange inhuman sounds that they wanted investigated; several came running up because huge rats were in their cabins (it only took one boy to "see" a rat for all the boys in his cabin to have seen it too); still others were sure a monster was on the roof or prowling in the bushes; four boys woke screaming with nightmares, and two wet their beds.

The following morning the boys were already assembled in the rec area for the breakfast trek to the mess hall when I appeared with Mo. Immediately they fell silent. "Form a line of twos," I said. They quickly fell in. Mo and I led the way as they silently trudged along behind us. They didn't quite know what to make of me—whether I was a sorcerer or a madman—but they were clearly intent on staying in line and not taking any chances.

Chapter 8

A COPPERHEAD'S BITE IS A WHOLE
LOT WORSE THAN ITS BARK

Bud Fischer, the nature counselor, had captured a copper-head, which he kept in a secure wire cage. Chief Berman assembled the entire camp at the lakefront to have a look at the snake and to hear Bud tell about its habits and characteristics. The campers all sat on the slope going down toward the lake and Bud stationed himself and his copperhead between them and the water.

Bud said that in no circumstance was anyone to try to capture a copperhead, as he had done, because they were very fast and deadly and only an expert should try to handle them. He assured everyone that the snakes were very unlikely to go into the cabins or assembly areas and would most likely keep to their own terrain. But, he said, copperheads were aggressive and unpredictable, and might attack a person who unwittingly came too near to them.

Bud wanted everyone to know what the procedure was if bitten by a copperhead. The wound had to be lanced immediately, the poison removed, and anti-toxin serum administered. Bud said that the serum was on order and should arrive within a few days. It would be kept in the icebox in the infirmary and the sooner it was administered, he said, the better.

"The most important thing you can do if bitten," Bud told us, "is to lie still, because the more your blood circulates, the more the poison is carried through your body. All counselors have first-aid kits that have scalpels and suction cups in them and they should immediately lance a cross through the bite marks, causing the wound to bleed, and then draw out the bloody poison with the suction cup. Of course, if you are on a hike or somewhere where the first-aid kit is not handy, then use a pocket knife to make the cuts and suck out the wound. But be careful—if you have a cut or sore in your mouth, it's possible you will get the poison into your system that way, so let someone else suck out the wound.

"Now I'm going to let this copperhead out of its box so that you can see what it looks like and how it moves."

There was a loud stir among the campers at the front of the assemblage.

"Don't be concerned," Bud said. "I'll have him under control and after you've all seen him, I'm going to whack his head off."

Bud picked up a long forked stick which he had leaned against the cage, and with his left hand he took hold of a rope which was attached to a snap lock on the front of the cage. He stationed himself beside the cage, pulled up on the rope which released the lock. As the cage door swung open, the snake wriggled a short distance out of the cage, then stopped to reconnoiter. Bud quickly and adroitly stabbed the fork of the stick just behind the snake's head, pinning him to the sand. The copperhead immediately lashed himself around in a violent attempt to get free, but Bud kept his head firmly pinned, only the

59

snake's body being free to wriggle.

Bud said it was one of the biggest copperheads he had ever seen, and one of the strongest. He suggested that the campers line up and pass by in single file to get a good, close look at the snake so that they could readily identify it. The first campers in line passed by at a distance of ten or twelve feet, but by the time our group took its turn the distance had been reduced to an intrepid four feet.

It's hard to say exactly what happened, it happened so fast, but just as Mo Brennan approached the snake with his group, which included my brother, the copperhead wriggled free from Bud's forked stick, whipped around, and struck Bud twice in his left ankle. Bud yelled out a warning. Mo picked up the two kids who were in the vicinity of the snake and literally threw them out of the way, then he pulled back his right foot and gave the copperhead a terrific kick that sent it flying toward the water. Mo then grabbed the stick and pinned the stunned snake to the ground while others of us rushed the cage over to him and helped get it back in.

All attention now turned to Bud Fischer, who was sitting on the ground. Chief Berman ordered all campers to return to their cabins immediately. Bud had taken out his pocket knife and now he made several rather deep cuts right through the bright red dots left by the snake's fangs. Blood came gushing out. Mo was all set to start sucking out the poison, but one of the counselors, whose cabin was nearby, came running down the incline with his first-aid kit. He gave the suction cup to Bud, who started to use it immediately. The nurse had not come to the demonstration, but someone had gone to fetch her. Bud told Babe Halpern to use his handkerchief and make a tourniquet at the calf of his leg to keep the poisoned blood from spreading.

"We've got to get some serum," Bud said to Chief Berman.

"As soon as possible. I took an awfully big shot."

Chief Berman told Babe to take the small truck and get to Bagnell or Camdenton as fast as he could.

"Do you know anyone who's got it there?" Babe asked.

"No," the Chief said, "just ask around."

"What makes you think there is any?"

"Because this is copperhead country."

Bud suddenly lay back on the ground and put his arm over his eyes. Mo took the suction cup and began working it.

"I'm cold," Bud said.

Someone ran up for a blanket.

"I'm going over to the Girl Scout camp," Chief Berman said. "They just may have some." He ran down to where the camp's outboard was tied to the dock. It wouldn't start. Murphy, the swimming counselor, ran down to help.

I turned my attention to Bud Fischer. He was shivering, but there were drops of perspiration on him. Mo kept working the suction cup. We covered Bud securely with the blanket and tried to raise the upper portion of his body so he'd be lying on a slant toward his feet. The nurse, a husky, middle-aged, brusque woman, arrived with a black medical bag, but there wasn't much she could do besides paint around the wound with some antiseptic.

Bud's arm fell away from his face as he lapsed into unconsciousness. His face was very white and cold. The nurse took his pulse and listened to his heart and looked worried. Nobody said a word. There were eight of us there, but not a word was spoken.

The outboard started up with a roar, and, with Murphy at the controls, the boat sped away from the dock. I figured it would take them about twenty minutes to get to the Girl Scout camp. I had never seen anyone die, or anyone dead, but from what I had seen in movies and read in books, Bud looked like he was dying and I was very frightened. It seemed so unreal not to be able to do anything. I watched Bud's chest, but I could not detect any breathing.

I was the first one to speak. "Is he dead?" I asked the nurse.

"No," she said.

"How bad is he?"

"Bad."

There wasn't much blood coming out of the wound because of the tourniquet, so the nurse took it off. Right away the flow of blood increased.

"Won't that release the poison through his body?" Mo asked.

"Yes," the nurse answered, "but we've got a lot of the poison out by now."

"But some of it is in him, isn't it?"

"Yes."

"Isn't that serious?"

"Yes."

"Might he die?"

"We need the serum."

We could still hear the boat put-putting across the lake. It was a small outboard motor and although they were going as fast as they could, they weren't going very fast.

We got more blankets and tried to make Bud more comfortable. Every once in a while the nurse would raise one of Bud's eyelids and peer at his eye. She never changed her expression. Some campers came sneaking down to have a look and we ran them off. We learned that before leaving for Bagnell, Babe had telephoned the doctor there but he was on a case in Eldon.

I had not thought much about death. No member of my family had died, and only once had I been to a funeral. (When I was nine years old, two kids with whom I had been playing had been buried in a mud slide and one of them died, but I wasn't there when the firemen dug out his body.) Also, it seemed unreal that anyone as big and strong and athletic as Bud could suddenly be leveled like this from a mere snakebite. I felt sick to my stomach and very conscious of my own breathing.

The nurse took a hypodermic out of her bag, filled it with something, and gave Bud an injection in his arm. After a few minutes he moved his head a little and made some kind of sound. Then he opened his eyes, just briefly, and closed them again. The nurse slapped his cheek several times and tried to rouse him by calling his name, but he didn't open his eyes again.

Mo was the first one to hear the returning motorboat. All of us, except the nurse, went down to the dock. We stood there in a line on the dock watching the boat enlarge as it headed toward us. There was no way to know if they had the serum or not because they'd be coming back in just about the same length of time. I couldn't get rid of the sick feeling in my stomach.

The boat seemed to return much faster than it had departed, and now, as it neared the dock, we could see why. It was a larger boat with a more powerful outboard. There were three people on board, Murphy, Chief Berman, and the nurse from the Girl Scout camp.

The boat roared up to the dock. We helped the nurse onto the dock and, clutching her bag, she ran with us to where Bud was lying.

She opened her bag and began taking things out; the two nurses worked together without saying a word. From the careful way she was filling a hypodermic from a small bottle, I knew it had to be the serum. Our nurse was rubbing alcohol on the crook of Bud's right arm, preparing him for the injection. The

63

Girl Scout nurse held the hypodermic up to the sky and squirted a little of the serum, then she slid the needle into Bud's arm and slowly emptied the contents of the chamber.

"You know something?" Chief Berman said. "They just received it this morning. A girl was bitten last week and they had to take her all the way back to St. Louis."

"He'd have never made it," our nurse said.

The Girl Scout nurse took Bud's pulse and his blood pressure and listened to his chest with her stethoscope.

"I think we can move him," she said. "But try to keep him as steady as possible."

We didn't have a stretcher in camp, but we made one out of two poles and a couple of jackets, putting the poles through the jacket sleeves. Then we lifted Bud very carefully and carried him up the incline to the infirmary. We went slowly and tried not to jiggle him. Once or twice he made a little sound, but he was still unconscious when we left him in the infirmary.

I didn't eat any dinner that night and I barely slept at all. It was just getting to be dawn when I quietly let myself out of the cabin and went up to the infirmary. The light was on. Through the window I could see Bud sitting up in bed. One of the nurses was sitting beside him. He was holding a cup and sipping something hot. I would have gone in and talked to him, but for some reason I began to cry. It was maybe the third time in my life I had cried. I couldn't understand why.

I went back to my cabin and fell asleep immediately. As it turned out, that entire summer, the only person bit by a snake was Bud Fischer.

Chapter 9

WHOA THERE, DICKY BOY! THE
HEAD COUNSELOR IS PULLING THE
REINS. WHOA! DAMMIT, WHOA!

I was able to elude detection as a non-swimmer by staying away from the waterfront. Having established myself as the camp's Indian authority, I had such a full program involving Indian songs, makeup, costumes, dances, ritual, and crafts that I easily fobbed off waterfront activity onto the other counselors. I was even supervising teepee and totem-pole projects. Of course, I knew absolutely nothing about any of these activities, but neither did anyone else. The combination of my imagination and the camp's gullibility made my life a heap big cinch.

For instance, I had never heard an Indian song in my life, but one of my Indian books contained a few lines of an Indian chant which I expanded by using the same rhythm and inventing some words which were in the vein of the ones in the book. This is what I came up with:

Kili, kili, kili, kili,
Watch, watch, watch, watch,

Kay you kim kum kaw-wah.
Kili, kili, kili, kili,
Watch, watch, watch, watch,

Kay you kim kum kaw-wah.
Hay, ha-a-cham-wah,
Hay cham-wah polly-wam-ba,
Hay ha-a-cham-wah,
Hay cham-wah,
Polly-wam!

I made up some music to go with the words, and asked Corny to write down the notes for me so that Blanche Marlies, who ran the camp's office, could play it on the piano. I claimed it was a song I had learned from a St. Louis Indian who had gone to Soldan High with me. I taught the song to the Indian Mound campers and when Chief Berman heard them sing it he immediately decreed it to be the official camp song.

But I could not generate much enthusiasm among the boys for my Indian program because of the truculent resistance of Horse Face. He wouldn't put on war paint, try to dance, wear a loincloth, or sing a note of "Kili, Kili, Kili." I tried to explain about Indian braves and how, if he'd let me, I'd make him up as the fiercest warrior in the tribe.

"Not me," he said. "I don't wanna go around singin' and dancin' with lipstick on my face and wearin' a diaper."

"It's not a diaper—it's a loincloth."

"Call it what you want, it's a diaper."

"If it's a diaper, how come I'm wearing one and all the other counselors?"

"Maybe you *need* diapers, how do I know?" That got a great laugh out of the campers.

"Take off your pants and put on this loincloth," I commanded.

"No, there's no one gets my pants off."

Mo made a move toward him.

"I'll write my old man that you fruits are trying to get my pants off."

"All right—tell you what," I said, "wear the loincloth over your pants."

He hesitated. "All right, but none of that girl stuff on my face. I got a bad enough puss without all that gunk smeared on me."

"It's not girl gunk," I said. "Look, it's paste from red berries —just like the Indians used."

Horse Face covered his face with his arms. "Get away with that! I don't wanna be no goddam Indian!"

As I said, Horse Face's vociferous opposition put a decided damper on my attempt to turn the rest of the campers into an Indian tribe. I tried to tempt Horse Face with a really lethal-looking tomahawk that Corny made in his crafts shop, but that didn't work either. There was no way we were going to get him to decorate his face and wear a loincloth. He had been called Horse Face all his life and he wasn't about to do anything that would call attention to his physiognomy.

I was brooding about this while thumbing through one of my Indian books when I came upon a section devoted to the medicine man. On the page was an illustration showing a medicine man in full regalia—ferocious-looking, bizarre mask with a huge bird beak, jutted teeth, and wild, disarrayed hair; he wore a brightly decorated robe that reached the ground, and he was brandishing a fur-covered mace with dangling feathers. A-ha, I thought, the perfect lure for Horse Face—a ferocious mask to cover his face, a long robe to cover his body, and a lethal weapon to attack evil spirits. If Horse Face basically does not like being Horse Face, I reasoned, then this should be the answer to his Indian conversion.

I gave the medicine-man picture to Corny, who made a papier-mâché mask even more ferocious and bizarre than the pictured one. My Indian crafts workshop created a robe out of burlap sacks which we painted and beaded, and we made a wooden mace that we covered with painted toweling and chicken feathers.

I sent for Horse Face, and when he entered the rec hall, there I was in the middle of the room, in the medicine-man regalia. I strode toward him with a deliberate stalking step, and Horse Face didn't know whether to run from this menacing monster or hold his ground. When I was a few feet away, emitting animal sounds, he bolted for the door.

"Horse Face!" I shouted. "Wait a minute!"

He stopped.

I took off the mask. "Come here."

He slowly walked back to me. I put the mask and robe on him, and handed him the mace. I then steered him over to the window where he could see his reflection.

"Gom! Gom!" he grunted, a perfect sound for his new face.

"You are Shwani, the medicine man, healer of arrow wounds and procurer of rain."

"Gom! Gom!" said Horse Face.

"You cook magic potions and send magic smoke into the air."

"Gom de gom!" said Horse Face, and my Indian program was off the ground.

After that, when we had our weekly all-camp fireside pow-wow, each camper wore a chicken feather on his brow affixed with a rubber band and sang "Kili, Kili, Kili" while shaking his fists to the rhythm. To crown this tribal rite, I taught ten of my campers, my brother being one of them, to do a dance that I invented to go along with the song. It consisted primarily of vertical hops and horizontal bends at the waist with the arms extended over head. Of the ten, Sullivan was by far the best Kili dancer and it occurred to me that perhaps there was something hereditary about terpsichore. But on added reflection I realized that the closest my father got to dancing was tapping his foot when the rhythm got hot.

The Indian costumes we used consisted simply of loincloths (towels) held up by a piece of rope around the waist. But when it came to war paint, that's where I excelled. At the start, I copied face markings I found in one of my books, but soon I began to embellish those and became more and more creative as I discovered my flair for face decoration.

My success as the Indian expert from St. Louis gave me such a heady me-heap-big-brave-Indian illusion that I decided, one day, to mount the camp's one horse, Dicky Boy. I had never been on a horse before, but I had seen Dicky Boy trotting around the grounds with Chief Berman and others astride and there didn't seem to be anything to it. Attired in loincloth, feather, moccasins (made in the leathercraft shop), and full war paint, I got myself up on Dicky Boy, who realized, the minute I sat down in the saddle, that he had someone on his back who had never been on a horse before.

So Dicky Boy took off. Not terribly fast, but off. I pulled back on the reins, I jerked the reins, I shouted "Whoa!" and similar exhortations designed to make him stop, but he kept going at a steady pace, not very fast, just loping along, making a round of the four villages.

Since I did not want the whole camp to know about my predicament (and thereby lose my Indian standing), I stopped yelling "Whoa!" and "Ho there, you jerk!" and simply smiled as bravely as I could as we endlessly made round after round through the villages. At first no one paid much attention, since Dicky Boy was a common sight, but along about the eighth or ninth time I came clopping through the villages I could tell my tours were beginning to be eyed with some suspicion. I tried pulling Dicky Boy's ears, his mane, hitting him on the head with my fist, but nothing I could do or yell in his ear had any effect whatsoever on Dicky Boy's duly appointed rounds. On my eighth tour through Bear Village one of the counselors yelled, "Look out, here comes Paul Revere!"

I had considered sliding off, but I didn't quite have the guts to jump from that height at that speed. But that did seem to be the only reasonable solution even though it meant that Dicky Boy would run free, perhaps run away, and I'd be held accountable for that.

It was Sullivan who ultimately rescued me. He suddenly appeared, running alongside me.

"You stuck?"

"He won't stop."

"Pull the reins."

"I did. I am."

"He just keeps running?" Sullivan was having trouble keeping up.

"I've got to get down," I said desperately. "My can is awful sore."

"Put your hands over his eyes."

"Do what?"

"Get up on his neck and cover up his eyes."

I shinnied forward and, clamping my legs desperately, stuck the flats of my hands over Dicky Boy's eyes. He immediately jammed on the brakes. I slid down, holding on to the reins. Sullivan ran over and helped me walk the horse back to his stable.

"You ever been on a horse?" I asked him.

"Nope."

"Then how'd you know that about covering his eyes?"

"I read once that that's how they lead horses out of fires. I even saw it in a movie. I know I'd stop running if someone covered my eyes. Wouldn't you?"

Just because I was able to avoid swimming didn't mean I avoided it altogether. After dinner, just before it got dark, when there wasn't an evening program and the lakefront was deserted, I would sneak down to the water with Sullivan to teach myself how to swim.

There was a crib there, designed for beginners, that was made of wooden slats and set into the water at a depth of three feet. Sullivan stayed on shore as my lookout, to warn me if anyone approached, while I tried, night after night, to get my feet off the bottom of the crib. That was my problem. I would put my face in the water and pick up one foot, but to release *both* feet and execute a dead man's float was beyond me. Also, the second I immersed my face in the water, I began to get an anxiety about breathing. Holding my breath outside of water, I was right up there with the best of them (a bunch of us at the Forest Park tennis courts used to have breath-holding contests), but when I put my face in water, ten seconds was about my bursting point. Just the feel of the water on my face set off a terrible fear in me that somehow the water would seep up my nose and choke me.

I finally got to the point where I could hold on to the side of the crib with my face in the water and kick my feet, but that was because I had the security of holding on. When I tried the same thing in the center of the crib, away from the side, both feet just wouldn't come up.

Occasionally I tried to help Sullivan, whose swimming problems were similar to mine, only more so. I'd try holding him on the surface by putting both hands under his stomach, but I could never get him to put his face in the water. I'd hiss angry, deprecatory things in his ear, telling him he was a coward, chicken, a baby, but it didn't help. He would strain his neck as high up as he could, and with one hand he'd hold tight on to one of my arms. In the process, he'd thrash around considerably, and his breath came in short, whimperish huffs and puffs. Sullivan displayed more acute fear than I did, but as swimming duds we were equal.

On our trudge back from these abortive swims, we never spoke a word. Sullivan was usually pissed at me for the way I had spoken to him; I was invariably angry and depressed, for I had been thinking all day about how that night I was finally going to float on the surface, how I was going to get those legs up and stretch those arms forward and put my face in the water and *float*. No one could say that I did not think positive all day long, but it had no effect whatsoever on my legs. I'd hop around a little, but I had no confidence that if my feet left the security of the wooden planks on the bottom of the crib, my body would stay on the top of the water. I also lectured myself on how little risk there was of drowning, since even if I sank to the bottom I was only in three feet of water and could easily stand up, but that also did absolutely no good. I have previously described my phobia about water; no amount of practice and thinking was going to overcome its leadening effect.

One evening, after we had gloomily returned from still another frustrating crib attempt, my brother appeared at my cabin door and asked to speak to me. I stepped outside.

"It's about Horse Face," he said.

"Oh, not that again!" I was on my third broom with Horse Face and I was in no mood to take him on.

"That isn't what I mean," Sullivan said.

"What isn't what you mean?"

"It isn't about Horse Face and *me*, it's just about Horse Face."

"What about Horse Face?"

"I want to get his bayonet."

"Sure, that's all I need, for you to run around with a bayonet."

"Not for me—I want it for Horse Face."

"Are you nuts? With his temper? You want to get stuck through the gizzard?"

"No, listen, let me have it. He won't hurt me with it."

"Sullivan—what the hell is this all about?"

"Well, I was just walking back to my cabin and I heard this noise in the trees there that sounded like somebody was in there, so I snuck over and had a look and it was Horse Face leaning there against a tree and he was, well, kind of, you know, crying."

"Horse Face? You sure it was Horse Face?"

"I was gonna walk away because, you know, crying is private, but I sometimes get pretty sad. . . ."

"Do you go off and cry like that?"

"Sometimes. I *used* to more than now. Anyway, I went on over to Horse Face and asked him what was wrong. First he didn't want to tell me, but I just hung around and he finally stopped crying and then he told me. About his father. What he said was that his father was in the war and got hurt very bad when the Germans used gas. His father can't work. Sometimes he's in the soldiers' hospital and sometimes he's able to come home. He's in the hospital now and he's very sick again and, you see, that bayonet belonged to Horse Face's father. I really think it'd be nice if he could have it back. I think he just sort of wants to *have* it, you know, to sort of, well, *have* it."

I gave the bayonet to Sullivan to take back to Horse Face. I suddenly felt very bad about all those broomings. Wouldn't it be strange, I thought, if Horse Face was the one who would become Sullivan's friend? I wondered what a man was like who had been gassed. I had thought of gassing as inevitably fatal. It had never occurred to me that there could be permanently damaged survivors—blind, perhaps, mentally twisted, paralyzed. Of course, that explained Horse Face. Poor Horse Face. In a way, he and Sullivan had much in common. Yes, it would be funny if Horse Face turned out to be the friend that Sullivan was seeking.

Chapter 10

WHY DO THEY GIVE YOU A SHOT
BETWEEN THE EYES WHEN WHAT YOU
NEED IS ONE IN THE ARM?

One of the best things about the summer was being able to talk about college with those counselors who were already going to such places as Washington University, Missouri, St. Louis U., Rollins School of Mines, and Northwestern. I had been to the Washington U. campus only once, but that one visit had engendered a queasiness that had made me want to ask questions about this new, mysterious life every chance I could.

Washington U. is located in the heart of St. Louis, but, situated as it is on high ground that gradually rises up from Skinker Boulevard, it gives the illusion of being somewhere off by itself. When I got off the streetcar on Skinker and looked up the long, elevated walk toward the fieldstone building that stood majestically and gracefully atop the hill, I felt both uplifted by its beauty and comforted to discover that it was no bigger than Soldan High.

But when I reached the summit, which was an archway that transected the building, and looked beyond, I was disheartened to see that this first-glimpsed building was but one side of a quadrangle of buildings that enclosed a grassy expanse of shrubs and trees. And that beyond this quadrangle lay scores of other buildings, each one the size of Soldan High.

As I stood there, bewildered by this discovery, classes let out and an overwhelming flood of students was disgorged into the enclave of the quadrangle; this mass of students made me aware, for the first time, of how severe the competition for survival would be. Our home teacher at Soldan had told us what percentage of the university freshman class flunked out, and that was partly why I was disturbed (but only a small part, for I had too much confidence in myself to fear flunking out). What primarily bothered me was that with such an army of students, how could I achieve in college what had come so easily and effectively in high school?

At Soldan I had been an over-achiever, in scholastics, sports, and such extra-curricular activity as editing the newspaper, writing and performing in plays and musicals, playing in the school orchestra, captaining the debate team, representing the school in oratorical contests. These achievements, and the recognition that went with them, counterbalanced the squalid conditions of our home life and were, in a sense, necessities for me. But the sight of those hundreds of students pouring into the quad convinced me that I would be nothing more than a tadpole in this pond.

I was also disturbed by the students themselves. They were so well dressed and sophisticated. Many of the boys wore suits and neckties, pork-pie hats, saddle shoes, and tweed sports jackets. Soldan High wasn't in a suit-and-necktie district, and outside of graduation, I don't think I ever saw anyone my age wear a necktie. (If they had, someone would undoubtedly have snipped it off him.) The Washington U. girls were also much better dressed and prettier and worldlier than the Soldan girls, and their breasts were bigger. They wore pearls and cashmere sweaters and most of them walked across the campus with boys, whereas Soldan girls mainly walked with girls.

I never had a girl in high school, mostly because I didn't have money to go on dates. Or clothes. But to be perfectly honest, I also had a terrible inferiority about girls. I thought of them as having different feelings than I did; and I thought of myself as singularly unattractive. No girl had shown any aggressive interest in me that would have disabused me of this conception, so I submerged myself in schoolwork and let my lively fantasies take care of my yearnings for those girls whom I was attracted to but much too inhibited to approach.

My meeting, that day, with the Washington U. Scholarship Committee went very well. I was told that I would be granted a full scholarship, but the presiding Dean warned me that such a grant would not include the additional money needed for books, supplies, laboratory fees, meals, et cetera, and that I would have to supplement the scholarship with a job that would provide the extra money. I figured that my Hiawatha earnings would get me started, and I had hopefully applied for a NYA job which, if I got it, would take care of me the rest of the way. The National Youth Administration was a new government organization set up by Franklin Roosevelt to assist college students with jobs that were to be created on campuses and paid for, at the rate of fifteen dollars a month, out of federal funds. That wasn't enough to buy clothes, but it was just about enough for everything else, providing I brought my lunch.

The more I talked with those counselors at Hiawatha who were going to college, however, the more my fears about Washington were allayed. Not that they made me feel I would have an easy time of it—to the contrary, they all warned me of the perils of the transition from high school to college, a transition from relatively small classes with teachers who knew your name to huge lecture halls presided over by professors who read you their gospel and would have no personal contact with you from one end of the semester to the other. But what Bud Fischer and Mo and Babe and the others did make me aware of was that each year the seniors, a fourth of the student body, departed and that there was inevitably room for those freshmen who were able to endure and advance.

I thought about college a great deal; all the time, really. For years—all of high school and even before that—I had feared that because of our poverty I would not be able to go beyond high school. From the time I was ten, our life had been a struggle to survive, to elude creditors, landlords, and social workers who came around periodically to investigate the status of my brother and myself. A family that cannot put eight cents' worth of gray-fatty hamburger on the table for dinner is not a family that can likely produce seven hundred dollars tuition for college.

But my fantasy about going to college had been undaunted by the hamburger realities, and in my heart I somehow knew that when the time came I'd make it.

I go into all this to help explain my reaction when Mo Brennan appeared as usual with the Indian Mound mail for the daily mail call. Outside of an every-other-day letter from my mother, and a postcard from a girl I used to play tennis with in Forest Park, I had received no mail until Mo handed me this letter from Washington University. It had been sent to my home address and forwarded. I turned it over to see if, as always, my father had opened the flap of the envelope and read the letter. My father and I had fought this letter-opening battle for a long time. No matter how I yelled and screamed at him, he was compulsively attracted to my mail—all mail—and all he would ever say in response was, "What have you got to hide from your own father?" To my surprise, it looked like for once he had resisted the impulse to jimmy open the flap on the Washington U. envelope. I sat down on my cot to read the letter:

> Dear Sir:
>
> We regret to inform you that in the apportionment of our funds for scholarship assistance in the oncoming scholastic year, we find that our funding is insufficient to include you in the 1936–1937 program.
>
> However, if you wish to apply again for the following academic year, in the spring of 1937, we shall be pleased to give your application prompt consideration.
>
> Yours sincerely,
> Lionel R. Bunting
> Registrar

I sat there on my cot like someone had drilled me between the eyes with a .22. I could feel the blood running from my veins; my mouth went dry, and I was sick to my stomach.

Mo said something, but I didn't hear him. He came over and poked his forefinger against my chest. "Hey, what's with you? You're white as a nun's ass."

I didn't have the strength to talk, or even to hand him the letter. He took it from my limp hands and read it.

"I'll be a son of a bitch! I'll be a no good son of a bitch! Listen, they can't do that! It's too late—you haven't got time to do anything now, for Christ sake!"

It was just "Dear Sir," a form letter—that seemed to bother me more than anything.

"You get a lawyer—my uncle's a lawyer."

Paul Roth had come into the cabin on his way to play chess

with Babe Halpern. Mo gave Paul the letter.

"That's the trouble with having to depend on other people for money," Paul said. "Can't you get it from one of your relatives?"

"My father used up all our relatives by 1933," I said.

"Well, can't he borrow the money from the bank or someplace?"

I just said no. I couldn't explain to someone like Paul that no one will lend you money if you have no visible assets. Or invisible, for that matter.

For the rest of that day I just lay there on my cot, staring at the ceiling, not moving, not even my eyeballs. I had suffered a kind of total paralysis. I sent Corny to look after my activities.

Well, I thought, that's that. I'll try to get a job, but next year they'll write me again: "Dear Sir." I'll probably be getting that form letter every summer for the rest of my life.

I didn't go to dinner—I couldn't have eaten if they had paid me. Heavy knocks like this invariably hit me in the mid-section. I had so involved my future existence with going to Washington that I could not even imagine what life would be for me in the fall. I had no working experience or skill; and with most everyone unemployed I could not see anyone hiring me. My ambition, as far back as I could recall ambition ("And what do you want to be, little man?"), had always been to be a trial lawyer like Clarence Darrow. I had read everything about Mr. Darrow and sometimes I would look in the mirror and address the jury the way he did. When I debated for Soldan (we won the city championship) I was Clarence Darrow all the way. But to make it to the actual courts I had to have a law degree and "Dear Sir" had put an end to that dream. There used to be ways of getting admitted to the Bar without going to law school, as Darrow himself had done when he was young, but those days were long gone. And so were my hopes now.

I don't think I slept much, if at all, that night, but with the dawn of the new day came a slim ray of hope in the person of Babe Halpern. He had heard about my scholarship knock and came to the cabin to tell me about a private organization in St. Louis that had helped him through Mizzou.

"It's too late for this year, of course," he said, "but you should call the head of the organization and make an appointment to see her."

He gave me her name, address, and phone number: Mrs. Irwin Bettman, Scholarship Foundation, St. Louis. I called her that morning from the phone in Big Chief Berman's office (he was out) and told her I was interested in trying to get one of her scholarships. She said to come and see her. I didn't tell her that I needed the scholarship immediately. I decided it was better to spring that on her in person. Also, I didn't ask for a specific appointment because I knew it would be too far off.

I found out that the truck was going into St. Louis for supplies that afternoon, so I told Berman I had to go along to pick out some vitally needed Indian materials. The minute we hit St. Louis, I jumped the truck and went straight to Mrs. Bettman's address on Waterman Avenue. A uniformed maid opened the door.

"May I see Mrs. Bettman, please?"

"Was she expecting you?"

"Well, sort of. She said to come see her."

"She is quite busy at the moment. . . ."

"I'll only be a few minutes. Just tell her and see if she has a few minutes."

The maid hesitated. I smiled at her and stood up as straight as I could.

"Who shall I say is calling?"

She went away with my name while I stood on the porch

outside the open door. It was a lovely big house with gardener-tended flowers lining the steps and potted plants all along the balustrade of the porch.

The maid returned and led me into a small sitting room. She said Mrs. Bettman would see me in a short while. I hoped she would hurry because my confidence was waning fast in these surroundings. The bravado with which I had stormed these Waterman Avenue parapets was deserting me even before Mrs. Bettman's appearance. I was beginning to feel self-conscious and foolish for having barged in to see her.

Mrs. Bettman was a tall woman, handsome and elegant, with a gracious calmness in her manner. I apologized of course for having appeared without an appointment, but I explained as quickly as I could about the disaster that had befallen me.

"That is certainly unfair on the part of the university," Mrs. Bettman said.

"I was just wondering—why I came to see you—if maybe you had one scholarship left over—maybe somebody who got one decided not to use it, or something like that."

Mrs. Bettman smiled and shook her head. "No, I'm afraid all our scholarships were given out last March. But we can certainly consider your application for next year. . . ."

"But next year . . . is so far away. And this is . . . Listen, Mrs. Bettman, going to college is something awfully important for me. I've really counted on it. I mean, there's nothing to live for if I can't go *now*. I know that sounds pretty melodramatic, but I've worked so darn hard all these years and now the kids with money who didn't do nearly as well as I did all go to college and I don't. Sure, I can wait a year and I guess I'll have to, but then going to college won't be the same."

I was having trouble controlling my lips, so I got up to go.

"I'm sorry I bothered you. I just had to try. . . ."

Mrs. Bettman put her hand on my arm. "Before you go," she said, "come with me for a moment—it can't do any harm."

I followed her through a hallway and into a large living room, where, to my amazement, there were three card tables with ladies sitting around them, playing bridge.

"It just so happens I'm having a bridge party for the executive committee of the foundation," Mrs. Bettman explained.

"Oh, my goodness—and I interrupted . . ."

"It's all right, I was dummy this hand."

The ladies had stopped playing and were looking in my direction. I wanted to crawl under the rug.

"Ladies," Mrs. Bettman said, "I've just had an emergency visit from this young man who had a scholarship from Washington U. that was retracted at this late hour because they've run out of funds."

There was a sympathetic murmur from the ladies.

"He's a head counselor at Camp Hiawatha and came all the way in to see me."

"Where did you stand scholastically, young man?" one lady asked.

"I was second in my class."

"What school?"

"Soldan."

"How old are you?" another lady asked.

"Sixteen."

"And you're a *head* counselor?"

"Yes, ma'am."

"Why is college so important to you?"

"Because . . . well, I don't want to sound immodest, but I want to go to law school because Clarence Darrow is getting old and we'll need someone to replace him."

"A commendable objective," Mrs. Bettman said. "I can promise you serious consideration when we give out our scholarships next year."

"I'm terribly sorry to have interrupted your bridge," I said. "I had no idea—but it was a pleasure meeting you. It makes me feel better knowing there's an organization like yours that helps out those of us who need help." I had had a lot of practice at getting on the good side of those whose favors I needed, and praise such as this fell from my lips as spittle from a baby's.

Before I left, Mrs. Bettman gave me an application form to take with me. On the way back to Hiawatha, jiggling around in the old truck, I did feel somewhat better even though college in the fall was as hopeless as it had been before I went to St. Louis.

Chapter 11

YOUR EYES ARE GETTING HEAVY
AND YOU WILL DO AS I TELL YOU!
WON'T YOU? *PLEASE!*

After Bud Fischer was released from the infirmary, he was never allowed to be alone. Wherever he went, whatever he did, a counselor had to be with him because he was prone to sudden faints. The Bagnell doctor who finally came to examine him said that it might be months before all the traces of the copperhead poison were out of his system, and until then the effect of the poison was such that he might keel over in a faint at any time.

And he did. The faint never lasted for very long, but you'd be walking along with Bud and he would suddenly crumple and fall to the ground, out cold. We were instructed, when this happened, to stretch him out, elevate his feet, and make sure he hadn't swallowed his tongue. After a few minutes he would stir, arouse himself, get right up, and continue walking as if nothing had happened.

One evening after Bud had walked back to our cabin with Paul Roth and me, Little Chief Babe Halpern dropped by to ask me to tell a ghost story at the next weekly powwow. Word of my success in scaring the wits out of the Indian Mound campers with "The Pit and the Pendulum" had traveled to Chief Berman, and this was to be a command performance for the entire camp.

"You should have heard him," Paul said. "As that pendulum with the blade on it got lower and lower, moving toward the center of the victim's body, I thought those kids would all pee in their pants. He had them absolutely hypnotized."

That's how we happened to get on the subject of hypnosis. Babe, as I previously mentioned, was a psychology major, and he had performed some experiments in hypnosis that he told us about. He told us how, under hypnosis, people could be made to perform intellectual feats and physical feats they otherwise would not have been capable of.

"You mean you can enlarge a guy's brain and his muscles?" Mo asked skeptically.

"No, it's not a matter of enlarging anything. Rather, it has to do with suspending some things—blocks, inhibitions, feelings. It's rather simple in hypnosis to suspend the feeling of pain or fear or addiction. And with post-hypnotic suggestion we can implant reactions which can last for years."

"Like what?"

"Well, any number of things. Biting fingernails, smoking, fear of height, nervous tics . . . We have instructed subjects in deep hypnosis to do something on a certain day and at a certain time four months later and they have done exactly as directed."

"You say 'we'—you mean you're a hypnotist?"

"We've been doing these experiments in abnormal psych. The professor is there, of course, but we perform the hypnosis."

"Can you do it to one of us?"

"I guess so, but you'd be resistive because I've told you all this and it would be hard to establish a position with you. There are eight degrees of hypnotism and you only get really interesting responses when you get to five or beyond."

My brother appeared at the screen door. He wanted a penny to buy some jawbreakers at the canteen.

"What about Sullivan there?" Mo asked. "He doesn't know anything about it."

Babe said he thought that Sullivan would be a relatively easy subject if he was willing.

"Do you mind if Little Chief Halpern hypnotizes you?" I asked Sullivan.

"What you say?"

"If he puts you to sleep."

"Heck no, I don't want to go to sleep. I want to go up and get some jawbreakers."

"You can go up in a few minutes. This is kind of a test to see if he can make you sleepy."

"Well, I'm not—so he'll lose."

"I'll give you a quarter if I can't put you to sleep," Babe offered.

Sullivan thought that over. He didn't have a penny to his name. "All right," he said, "but hurry up before they close the canteen."

Babe had Sullivan lie down on one of the cots, and told him to relax. Then Babe took a key ring with keys out of his pocket and, holding it by the chain, let it dangle in front of Sullivan's eyes.

"Now I want you to watch these keys very closely," Babe said, "just keep your eyes on these keys, keep watching them, and listen to me as you watch these keys moving back and forth, back and forth, watch the keys, back and forth, back and forth, now you're getting a little sleepy, watch the keys, your eyelids are beginning to get a little heavy. . . ."

Babe was talking in a low monotone, his inflections keeping rhythm with the moving keys. I knew, from the way I had seen Sullivan react to candles, that he would be easily hypnotized. If Sullivan was at a table on which a candle was burning, he couldn't take his eyes off the flame, and pretty soon he got glassy and if the flame wasn't extinguished Sullivan would close his eyes and fall asleep sitting at the table. It only took a few minutes of watching those keys for Sullivan's eyelids to begin to flicker and then drop shut.

"You are now asleep, fast, fast asleep," Babe said. "Your eyelids are stuck fast. You can't open them. Try. Try hard. You see? No matter how hard you try, you can't open your eyes."

Babe put away the keys. "He's hypnotized," he announced.

"Show us some tricks," Mo said.

"Don't think of this as tricks," Babe said. "I've simply induced an unconscious state and now I will impose myself on that unconsciousness and exert my will."

Babe stood up. "Sullivan," he asked, "can you hear me?"

Sullivan nodded yes.

"Good. Now I want you to get up and stand on one leg with your arms outstretched."

Sullivan did as directed.

"Your legs and arms are made of wood," Babe said, "and you are perfectly comfortable like this. You have no desire to move your arms and legs. You can stay like this for hours. You have no desire to put your leg down. Your arms are not tired. They are not going to get tired."

"He could be faking all this," Mo said.

Babe asked if Mo had a pin. Mo opened a drawer, scrounged around in it, found a needle.

"Now, Sullivan," Babe said, "I want you to open your eyes,

but you will see only what I tell you to see. Open!"

Sullivan opened his eyes.

"Good! Now I want you to think about your right arm. When I count to three your right arm will not feel anything. Nothing. It is made of wood, don't forget, and so you will not feel anything. Ready? One—two—three!"

Babe took the needle and jabbed it into Sullivan's outstretched arm. Sullivan didn't react at all. A little round of blood appeared over the needle prick. Sullivan continued to keep his one-legged balance.

Babe took some matches from his pocket and lit one. He moved the flame closer and closer to Sullivan's eyes until it was virtually searing his eyelids, but Sullivan did not even blink.

"Here," Babe said to us, "pass this piece of paper around and put down a number—five or six digits—with letters, if you want."

We passed the paper around.

"Now, Sullivan," Babe said, "I want you to listen carefully. I'm going to read you some numbers that I want you to remember. Then I'm going to tell you some things I want you to do." Babe slowly read off the list of numbers we had written down. Mine was 264176AB4Z. There were ten such numbers on the list.

"Sullivan," Babe said in a commanding voice, "when I say go, I want you to put down your arms and leg, go outside, get some water in the pitcher, pick up six stones, run to the rec hall and back, bark like a dog, do three somersaults, come back in here, and sit down at this table."

Babe said "Go!" and Sullivan did everything precisely as directed. After he had returned to the cabin, Babe put a piece of paper in front of him. "Now write down those numbers I read to you," Babe said.

Without hesitating, Sullivan wrote down a list of numbers. We compared them against the original sheet and there was only one mistake.

"You said you could plant some things that the subject would do later," I said.

"Yes, post-hypnotic suggestion."

"How about swimming? Tell him he can swim."

Babe told Sullivan that when he went down to the water the following day, he must jump in and swim. He told him how he'd kick with his legs and move his arms and hold his breath when he jumped in the water. While he was telling him all this, Sullivan made faint, jerky motions with his arms and legs and held his breath.

"What if I gave him some commands?" Paul asked.

Babe told him to try. Sullivan didn't react at all. Babe told Sullivan to close his eyes and Sullivan obeyed. "You see, he hears only me. If I told him that after he wakes his brother was not in the room, he wouldn't, *couldn't* see you even if you went over and put your arm around him. I have a very deep hold on his subconscious. He is definitely in the deepest kind of hypnosis."

"Well, you've sure made a believer out of me," Mo said. "Listen, what about my next chemistry exam? I have a hell of a time with chemistry. What about I get hypnotized and have all the formulas and equations read to me?"

"It might work if you knew what to do with them."

"I'm gonna come see you just before next year's finals."

"Well, I better wake up Sleeping Beauty," Babe said. "Sullivan, I'm going to count to three, and when I say *three*, I want you to wake up. Ready?" Babe counted to three, but Sullivan did not wake up. Babe repeated his instructions, again counted to three, but Sullivan did not open his eyes. Babe got irritated.

"Now, come on, Sullivan, snap out of it! When I clap my hands I want you to wake up. You're not sleepy any more. Your eyelids are not heavy. You are waking up. Open your eyelids. Awake! Wake up!" He clapped his hands. Two times. Three. Right in front of Sullivan's face. No response.

"For Christ sake," Babe said. "What is this?"

I moved over to the cot and knelt down beside my brother. "What the hell?" I said to Babe.

"Listen, take it easy," Babe said, obviously worried. "I've done this a dozen times and they always wake up."

He started all over again with his litany about Sullivan opening his eyelids and counting to three, but Sullivan did not react at all.

I felt a rise of panic. When I was a sophomore in high school, one of the fraternities hazed a boy—just an initiation prank, something they made him drink, I believe, but the boy went into a coma and, after ten days, died. I knew the boy—he was on the debating team with me. My panic about Sullivan embraced this memory; I reached in front of Babe and took Sullivan by the shoulders and shook him, calling out his name. Shook him hard. Slapped his cheeks. Quite hard. Nothing disturbed his deep sleep.

"We better get the nurse," Mo said and he went running out the door.

Babe kept talking to Sullivan, trying to awaken him in any way he could think of, but to no avail. Sullivan's face was white and rigid; he looked dead. I could not swallow. I put my fingers on his pulse—it was faint and slow, very slow.

The nurse, Miss Collins, came bustling in, carrying her bag. Mo had already told her what had happened. She shoved Babe out of the way and sat down on the bed beside Sullivan. She pushed up his lids and looked at his eyes. Then she put her head on his chest and listened. Afterward she opened her bag and took out the blood-pressure equipment. She watched intently as she pumped the blood-pressure bulb. My insides felt like I was dropping in a runaway elevator.

"I don't know a damn thing about hypnosis!" Miss Collins exclaimed.

"Well, let me tell you—" Babe started to say.

"And neither do you!" she snapped. She took out a hypodermic and shot something into Sullivan's arm. Then she waited several minutes before taking his blood pressure again. It was a cool night, but Babe was perspiring heavily.

Miss Collins stood up. "All of this boy's vital signs are way down," she said. "He doesn't react to stimulus. We'd better rush him in to see Dr. Eggerton in Bagnell. Let's just hope *he* knows something about hypnosis. If not, we'll have to keep right on going to St. Louis."

We carried Sullivan up to the main building, where the camp car was parked. I got in the back with him and the nurse. Babe drove and Mo sat beside him. I put my arm around Sullivan's limp body and held him against me. He felt very small. Babe drove down the narrow road at a breakneck speed. Occasionally the nurse reached over and took Sullivan's pulse. Each time I asked if he was all right. She didn't answer me. She was furious, and her fury extended to all of us. She was right. It was Babe's doing, but we had all condoned it—more than that, encouraged it. We were as much to blame, willing, eager spectators, as the perpetrator himself. Especially me. His brother. If I didn't have the sense to protect a small boy against this guignol, then who would? Some brother! I encouraged him and then watched him being treated like Pavlov's dog. Only Pavlov didn't get his dog into this kind of terrible trouble.

My lips were close to Sullivan's ear. The engine of the old car, going at that speed, made a great noise. No one would hear me. "Sullivan," I said, "Sullivan! Oh, please wake up, please! Sullivan. Sullivan. Please. Please! *Please!*" I talked to him like that most of the way to Bagnell, but he didn't hear a thing.

Dr. Eggerton was having a late dinner, but he came down to his office the minute we carried Sullivan in.

"He's in a hypnotic coma," Miss Collins said. "This fellow put him into a deep trance and couldn't get him out."

Dr. Eggerton gave Babe a withering look and ordered all of us out of the office except Miss Collins. We went to sit in the small outer office. Babe put his head forward and buried his face in his hands. I was too nervous to sit. I began to fantasize how I would break the news to my mother. I didn't want to tell her on the telephone. Of course I'd have to take Sullivan's body back to St. Louis, but I couldn't just arrive with no notice; I'd have to let her know beforehand. Maybe I'd telephone my father and let him tell her—no, he was always so bad about delicate things.

I stood at the window and watched the flickering jets of the gas streetlamps. Our family didn't practice praying, so I just said, God, please help him. He had nothing to do with this, God, so please help him. He's a boy who's had no fun.

We waited in that little office for over an hour. Finally the door opened and the doctor came out.

"Where did you learn about hypnotism?" he asked Babe.

"At school," Babe said, standing up, "in abnormal psychology. I've done it ten or twelve times."

"In class? With your professor present?"

"Yes, sir."

"Practicing on other students?"

"Yes, sir."

"Superficial hypnosis. But when you deal with children—
they're so vulnerable—don't you realize the deeper the hypnosis, the more difficult it is to handle the subject?"

"I do now."

"Well, you're not to practice any more of your hypnotism on
anyone at Camp Hiawatha."

"Don't worry, Doctor."

"What about my brother?" I demanded. The hell with lectur-
ing Babe when I didn't know about Sullivan.

"He's all right," Dr. Eggerton said. He opened the door and
led us back into his office. Sullivan was sitting on a chair drinking hot tea. He gave me his big missing-teeth smile.

I knelt down beside him and put my hand on his arm. "Are you
all right?"

"Sure—I'm fine."

"You know what happened?"

"The doctor told me. But all I know is I fell asleep."

"You don't remember learning some numbers and standing
on one leg?"

"I did that?"

"Or having a needle stuck in you?"

"Really? Where?"

"I'll tell you all about it tomorrow."

"Show me where I got stuck."

I tried to show him, but there wasn't a mark. He finished his
tea and we got up to go.

"Thank you with all my heart, Doctor," I said. "How much is
your bill?"

"It gets charged to the camp," Miss Collins said.

"Goodbye, little man," the doctor said to Sullivan, putting his
hand on top of his head.

"Goodbye, Mr. Doctor," Sullivan said. "And thank you for the tea."

The doctor smiled at him and we started to leave. Sullivan looked up at me, a worried look. "I guess I don't get that quarter, huh?" he asked.

Chapter 12

CHIN UP, PANTS DOWN, AND
THE MOSQUITOES BE DAMNED!

Mostly what the counselors talked about when they got together was girls. There was only one girl in the camp, Blanche Marlies, who was the secretary, but she had a boy friend who came down weekends from Sedalia. I enjoyed listening to all the girl talk because, as I said previously, I myself had never had a real girl friend. Nor had I ever had sex with one. I had played around with girls at parties and I daydreamed about sex a great deal, but the opportunity to get in bed with one had never presented itself.

At first I was amazed to hear the extent of the other counselors' sexual triumphs, but Mo, in his growly voice, put me straight: "You don't believe all this bullshit, do you? They're playing with themselves, that's all. That lunk in Mark Twain—what's his name?—Howley?—the one who spun out all that bullshit about spending the night with those two sisters—you can bet the only times he ever gets it out of his pants is to pee."

"You mean none of them has really laid a girl?"

"Oh, sure, *some* of them—but you can bet it's mostly the ones who don't talk. Like you. I don't hear you shooting off your mouth about all the dames you've bounced."

"Well, I haven't."

"Haven't what?"

"Bounced any."

"Not even one?"

"No, not really."

"What the hell you waiting for?"

"I just—well, haven't had the opportunity."

"Opportunity! You think they're going to come up and say, 'Please let's get in the back seat of your car and do it'?"

"Well, that's part of it—we don't have a car."

"I don't mean you *need* a car. Find yourself a bush or a back porch. Girls want to do it, but you got to push them into it."

"Do you do it a lot?"

"I used to—until I met Greta. Then I had eyes for no one else. Greta—well, she liked it, but it made her feel guilty and it would take her a month to get over it and ready to be persuaded again. But thank God that's over."

"Greta?"

"Yeah. We broke up the night before I left for camp. She was going off too, to be a counselor in a girls' camp, so I thought it was a good time to split up."

"What did Greta do?"

"What do you mean, what did she do? She went to school, like I do."

"Isn't that, uh, unusual?"

"What's unusual about going to school?"

"What I mean is, girls who do it are usually, well, waitresses or nurses or someone like that, aren't they?"

"What the hell are you talking about?"

"It's just that I hear nice girls from good families won't do it."

"Now listen, I'm a nice guy from a good family, right? I do it, it's okay, but if a girl has the same feelings I have and she does it, she's a scarlet woman, that it? The idiot American dream—to marry a virgin. Who the hell wants a virgin? Doesn't know anything, full of hang-ups, quotes her mother. The worst lay I ever had was a virgin. All she did was cry. Before, during, and after."

In the face of Mo's pique at my own virginal status, I was almost tempted, in justification, to divulge that I was really only sixteen, but then again I didn't know how he would react to having a head counselor above him who was his junior. But even at sixteen, based on the criteria of the other counselors, I should have long since made my sexual debut. I had come close a couple of times, but I knew that in Mo's eyes close was worse than total abstinence.

"Any guy who gets close," he had once expostulated to Corny, "and doesn't is either chicken or faggy."

Mo had received no letters (nor had he written any) until one arrived from Greta. It had been sent to his home address and forwarded to him. He was lying on his cot reading it during the rest period, when he suddenly shot upright. "Pin Oak! Listen, that Girl Scout camp across the lake, isn't that Pin Oak?"

"Pipe down, Brennan," Corny said. "I'm trying to practice." He was sitting on the edge of his cot, as usual, blowing silently into his horn.

"How do you like that? She's right across the lake!"

"Does she know you're here?" I asked.

"No, that spat we had, I didn't tell her anything."

"Is she trying to make up?"

Mo was too busy reading to answer. Corny accidentally blew a high note on his horn and we all jumped.

"I'm sorry! Sorry!" Corny recoiled at our stares. "I was just imagining this big riff and—"

"Right across the lake!" Mo exclaimed, jumping to his feet. He motioned to me to come outside; he led me toward the rec hall, beyond earshot of the cabin.

"Let's go over there tonight."

"Where? The Girl Scout camp?"

"Yeah."

"We'll never get permission—you know Berman."

"Screw Berman—we'll go on our own."

"You mean, not tell him?"

"What he doesn't know won't constipate him."

"But if he finds out, he'll can us."

"Not us. We're indispensable. Anyway, how's he going to find out?"

"You better go by yourself, Mo. I really need this job."

"I need you for the canoe. Besides, Greta may have a girl friend and you'll finally get fixed up."

"You mean you're going to do it in a *Girl Scout* camp to *Girl Scouts?*"

"I'd do it in a church to nuns, for crying out loud! Anyway, once they take off those dumb uniforms they're not Girl Scouts —they're female potatoes like all the rest. I'm going up and sneak in a phone call to Greta, and tonight we'll paddle us over to Pin Oak."

"Now, wait a minute, Mo—I'm not much of a canoe paddler...."

"Will you stop worrying? Cripes, no wonder you never get laid. Put your mind on what's important and everything else takes care of itself."

There was obviously no way I could turn Mo off. At eight o'clock he came to get me, and with a fearful sense of foreboding doom I followed him down to the lakefront, which was deserted. It was dusk. He put me in the bow of a canoe, showed me how to hold the paddle, untied the boat, stepped into the stern, and off we went.

Actually, paddling the canoe across the still, quiet lake in the dusk was a lovely experience. All I could hear were the shore birds settling in for the night and the sound of the paddles breaking the water. After a while I was able to stroke the paddle without splashing the surface. It was easy to navigate, since Pin Oak was the only installation on the opposite shore and its lights were clearly visible.

Mo had arranged with Greta to meet her on the shore a short distance away from the dock. As we neared the shore, a flashlight suddenly snapped alive and Mo headed for it. There was a clearing in the brush where it was easy to beach the canoe. Two girls were waiting there: the one with the flashlight was small, rather blond, with red cheeks and very white teeth. The other was, to put it quite simply, the most beautiful girl I had ever seen in my life—and that includes the movies. She had dark hair in a pony tail, violet almond-shaped eyes, and breasts that made a mockery of her Girl Scout blouse. The one with the flashlight was Greta.

"This is my friend Connie Firestone," Greta said to me after Mo had introduced us. Connie looked at me and smiled. I felt all my bones melt.

"We can't stay very long," Greta said, "because they may come looking for us."

"We brought a little snack," Connie said. She had a low voice with a whispery quality to it. They led us up the bank to a grassy spot where they had spread a blanket on which there were a cake and a thermos of lemonade. The gnats and mosquitoes were bad, but Greta passed around a bottle of citronella, which we rubbed on ourselves. Mo put his hand on Greta's thigh while he was eating his cake.

"I understand you're a head counselor," Connie said. She had long fingers with healthily pink nails bottomed with white arcs. The valley of her breasts showed above the top button of her Girl Scout blouse.

"He's our number-one Indian," Mo said, "and the best ghost man in camp. Sometime make him tell you 'The Pit and the Pendulum.' You won't sleep for a week."

"Oh, I absolutely adore ghost stories!" Connie exclaimed.

"Well, it's not really a ghost story—it's a horror story."

"Better still! Will you tell it?"

"Listen," Mo said, "Greta and I are going to take a little walk. You two make yourself comfortable on the blanket."

They left with the flashlight. "I'd feel pretty silly sitting here telling you a story," I said. I was having a little trouble breathing now that we were alone.

"Why did he want to take a walk?" Connie asked. "Just when we were all starting to have fun?"

"I guess they wanted to have—uh, to have a private talk."

Connie's violet eyes studied me. "Do you have a girl back home?"

"No, I . . . No."

"How come?"

"I wanted to keep the summer to myself." A pretty senseless remark, but I was having trouble keeping my head clear.

"I know what you mean!" Connie said, and I was grateful. "I did the same thing—cut off all my tangling alliances."

"Where do you go to school?"

"Stephens College in Columbia. I'm a sophomore. And you?"

"Washington University." What else could I say?

"Do you live in St. Louis?"

"Yes."

"I'll bet you never even *heard* of where I live—Chillicothe."

"I've *been* to Chillicothe."

"You haven't!"

"I went there once with my father when he had his jewelry line—to help him carry his samples."

"What did you think of it?"

"Prettiest main street I ever saw."

"Imagine your having been to Chillicothe! Do you think you'll come again?"

"No—my father lost his jewelry line."

"You know," Connie said, "it's chillier here by the water than I thought."

There wasn't a breath of air stirring, but I moved closer to her and put my arm around her. Just *barely* put it around her as if she wouldn't know it was there.

"I should have brought my jacket."

I put my arm around her more securely.

"Oh," she said, "I barely know you—but it does feel warmer."

If Mo had been sitting there instead of me, he would doubtless have pushed her back onto the blanket and tried to make out. But I just kept on talking as we both faced out to the lake. I let my hand fall a little down from her shoulder so that my fingertips touched the side bulge of her breast. She didn't object. We kept on talking. She had a wonderful laugh. I put my other hand on top of hers. The smoothness of her skin and the scent of her neck were emboldening me. I looked her full in the face. She turned her violet eyes to mine.

"Are you feeling warmer?" I asked.

"I'm fine now," she said.

I put my lips forward to kiss her, but she rolled her lips away from me and all I got was hair. I could hear Mo growl, "Take her face in your hands and *assert* yourself!" But instead I took my arm from around her and clasped my hands across my knees.

"Oh, don't be hurt," she said.

"I'm not hurt," I said in a hurt tone.

"Yes you are."

"I'm not."

"Come here. . . ."

She had turned to face me. I put my arm around her again and she put her lips against mine. It was so powerful, so exciting, so beyond anything I had ever experienced with a girl before, that I felt myself ready to have an orgasm. Whether I would have had or not was to remain unresolved, for at that moment, with our lips locked and her soft billowy breasts pressed against me, there was a great stirring in the underbrush, a thumping, whirring sound, as Mo came pell-mell out of the vegetation, his pants half on, half off.

"Come on! Let's go! Let's go!" he shouted at me as he headed toward the canoe.

I unwound myself from Connie and sprinted after him.

"What's wrong?" Connie cried. "What happened?"

"Run!" I yelled to her. "Run!" She got up and ducked out of sight.

Mo literally picked up the canoe and pitched it onto the water. We scrambled aboard; as flashlight beams began to appear on shore, Mo propelled the canoe with mighty strokes toward Hiawatha.

"Keep low so they can't see our faces," he whispered.

It is very difficult, I discovered, to paddle a canoe and keep low at the same time. From the shore now a cacophony of female voices was coming at us. When we got to the center of the lake, we rested.

103

"What the hell did you do?" I asked. I was panting heavily from the canoe dash.

"They caught me with my pants down."

"Greta too?"

"No, she escaped."

"They know who you are?"

"No—my ass was bare, but I covered my face."

"But they know you're from Hiawatha?"

"They'll surmise that. Maybe they'll line all of us up for an ass inspection. 'You mean, Madam, that you can make positive identification of Counselor Brennan's ass?' " Mo suddenly thought of something: "Have you got freckles on your ass? I've never noticed."

"I don't think so."

"Did you score with that Connie?"

"I was just getting into it when you broke everything up."

"What a luscious piece *she* is!"

I didn't want him to speak of her in those terms. "We better get ourselves back to camp," I said.

"Yeah. What did you think of Greta?"

"Terrific."

"I got mosquito bites all over my ass."

"Now, *there's* how they'll identify you—you should have used the citronella."

Mo laughed. "Listen, buddy," he said, "when Greta's ready there's no time for citronella."

Berman never found out just who violated the virgin shores of Pin Oak, but after that night the canoes were all padlocked together. The day after our visit Mo broke out with a terrible case of poison ivy in the intimate places you can imagine. He was in constant misery, especially when he had to walk or go to the bathroom. "If I could only think of some way not to piss," he lamented. He kept himself painted with calamine lotion, but it didn't do much good.

Greta wrote him a letter, which he showed me, to say that she had poison ivy so bad she was running a fever of 103 degrees. It was a sad letter. There were tear splotches all over the ink. Of course, if Charlie Chan or Dick Tracy had been put on the case, Mo would have been easily collared, but lucky for Mo (and me) Big Chief Berman never got wind of the incriminating coincidence of the two poison ivies.

It took Mo about ten days to get rid of his affliction; I guess it taught him a lesson because afterward he never again mentioned going across to Pin Oak or even getting laid.

During the course of the summer Connie Firestone wrote me several letters that she signed "Love"; I reread all of them almost every day. I wrote to her much more than she wrote to me, but I didn't mind. I rekissed her a thousand times, and had a thousand fantasies about what might have been if Mo hadn't come charging out of the underbrush. I'd never known anyone like Connie. I think I would have married her right then and there if I'd had the chance. I asked her to send me a picture of herself, but she never did. We promised to find each other after school started in the fall, either in Columbia or St. Louis—after all, Columbia was only a couple of hours from St. Louis and I wrote how I'd hop down there on the weekends. I was so far gone I gave no thought to how I would finance even a single such expedition. The only reality that intruded on me was the pall of having lost my scholarship—and the status of being a college man.

But thanks to Connie, a rather dormant part of me had been inflamed; wonderment had shifted to desire. I couldn't get her out of my mind. One evening, in the middle of a chilling bonfire performance of "The Tell-Tale Heart," I began to think about Connie and me on the blanket that night, and I completely blanked out on the heart which was beating a lively tattoo (courtesy of Corny) under the ground at my feet. There were a couple of minutes there while I fumbled around, making up things as I tried to get back on the track, that must have made poor Poe wince in his tell-tale grave.

Chapter 13

I'LL BET WHEN I'M DEAD AND GONE,
I *STILL* CAN'T DO THE DEAD MAN'S FLOAT

The camp did not hear about my brother's hypnotic coma because those of us who were party to it never mentioned it, and Miss Collins did not send a report to Big Chief Berman. We all liked Babe very much and we instinctively knew that if Chief Berman got wind of what Babe had done, he would fire him. Lucky for Babe, Berman had been across the lake at the Girl Scout camp when the ill-fated hypnotism had occurred. (Berman was visiting Rosemary McMartin, the Girl Scout directress, whom he had met that time he had gone for the snake serum.)

The day after the hypnotism Babe was full of concern about Sullivan, but there was nothing to worry about; Sullivan was in good fettle. In the morning wrestling session, he won his match, and Mo moved him up to number two on the flyweight ladder. Also, in the rec room that morning Sullivan found a Nehi bottle cap that had a winning twenty-five-cent mark under its inner lining. He came running into my Indian crafts room to show me his Nehi prize. The odds against finding a twenty-five-center were astronomical—in fact, finding *anything* under the Nehi bottle cap was pretty astronomical—and Sullivan was bubbling with excitement.

I asked him a few questions about the previous evening, but it was obvious that he recalled nothing; it was also obvious that he was none the worse for having endured the ordeal. Sullivan was beginning to enjoy camp and to shuck off the aura of morose detachment, of loneliness I guess you might say, that had always enveloped him. His unexpected prowess as a wrestler had given him a measure of confidence that he had never had before—albeit a tentative confidence, edged with a suspicion that it was not real—but without any element of cockiness.

My own feelings toward Sullivan were ambivalent: in one way I was happy to watch him beginning to respond to challenges he would never even have attempted before he came to camp. Sullivan was a non-participant who strenuously avoided any confrontation whenever he could. He had a ready excuse for not doing things, for not even *trying* to participate in any endeavor that involved competition. For instance, he did all right in school, studied just enough to get by, but he would never extend himself in a deliberate attempt to get a high grade for fear of not succeeding. If he only tried for a mediocre grade and received it, that satisfied him. Better to try for a little and achieve it than to try for a lot and fail.

When Sullivan started to wrestle, that was again his attitude, but Mo straightened him out right off the bat. For Mo, wrestling was a divine calling, and he inducted the campers into it like a holy order. From the moment they first set foot on the mat, Mo emphasized their assets rather than their shortcomings. He had a fine knack for making every boy feel that his quickness or his headlock or his body press was a remarkable achievement, and by the end of the first week there wasn't a boy in his class,

Sullivan included, who didn't have dreams of becoming the new Strangler Lewis or Jimmy Londos. At the end of each session Mo would reward those boys who had done particularly well with a star which he glued on the back of the boy's left hand. For a camper to be able to walk around Indian Mound Village with one of Mo's stars on his hand was a swaggering achievement.

On the day after his hypnotic coma, not only did Sullivan find a twenty-five-cent Nehi cap and receive one of Mo's stars, but a much greater good fortune befell him. It happened in the evening when we went down to the lake for another of my fruitless attempts to get waterborne. As usual, Sullivan sat on the edge of the dock as my lookout while I lowered myself into the crib, full of the high resolve I had worked up during the day, determined that this time I would really *do it*. I had just started my pathetic attempts to fulfill that resolve when I heard Sullivan say, "Listen, I'm coming in."

I looked up and saw him standing on the ledge of the crib. Without hesitating, he jumped in and began swimming toward the far end of the crib. I couldn't believe what I was seeing. Sullivan's fear of water, as I previously explained, was as pronounced as mine, perhaps more so, but here he was splashing his way down the length of the crib, no anxiety, keeping himself nicely on the surface even though his strokes were clumsy. He splashed his way back to where I was and stood up smiling.

"Why didn't I do that before?" he asked. "There's nothing to it."

"When— How did you— Who taught you to—"

"Nobody. I mean, I dunno. I really dunno. I was just sitting here and I felt like trying to jump in and swim. So I did. Listen, A, it's nothing. Honest. Just stand up here and jump in and you'll swim."

109

Babe's post-hypnotic swimming instructions! Although I had seen it with my own eyes, I still found it hard to believe that anything so difficult as swimming could have been achieved with Babe's abracadabra. It certainly shattered my rationalization that it was some kind of physical deficiency in a person that rendered him incapable of swimming. The inner ear, something like that, that was probably hereditary and afflicted all the offspring of a family. Sullivan was proof positive that a non-swimmer's only obstacle was fear. If only I could be hypnotized and shuck off my fear as easily as Sullivan had. That wouldn't be possible now that Babe had been put out of the hypnotism business. But I am sure that if Babe had not promised to stop hypnotism, I would have taken the risk of a coma in order to get the same post-hypnotic natatorial results as Sullivan. I would have risked more than that, so desperate was I to get my feet off the bottom of that goddam crib and float freely on the surface. It seemed so easy, the way Sullivan had done it. Not to be able to swim was such a disgrace, so cowardly.

Angrily, I grabbed hold of the side of the crib, took an extravagant breath, put my face in the water, got my feet up, and tried to shove myself away. But no sooner had my hands left the security of the wooden railing of the crib than I panicked as I always panicked. My head jerked up; coughing, my feet plummeted to the bottom. Coward.

As we walked back up the trail toward the cabins, I felt dejected and depressed and, to be honest about it, resentful of Sullivan. I don't particularly mean jealous, although at that moment I certainly envied his sudden-found ability to swim, but my resentment was really beyond jealousy. It had to do with his very presence, the responsibility of caring for him, and caring about him. And that's what I meant when I said I was ambivalent about him. Since the beginning of the Depression, when I was

110

ten, I had pretty much had to fend for myself, especially after we were reduced to living in that one room at the busted-down Avalon Hotel. I had to scrape and connive for everything I needed, from daily food to shoes for graduation from the Admiral Dewey grammar school. I even had to defend myself against my own father to keep him from unearthing my meager savings from their secret hiding place and plundering them.

In all this time, since Sullivan was mostly away with relatives, he was not an element in my life. Even on those brief occasions when he did return to live with us, I managed to exist around him, never involving myself in his existence at all. Out of necessity, I had learned to be self-sufficient, self-serving, and totally selfish. It was a way of life I had, by circumstance, been forced into, and it was comfortable, and in a real sense, this insecurity was my security.

But now Sullivan was no longer an itinerant who touched down for a moment without disturbing anyone or anything, only to disappear lightly without leaving any tracks. He was back for good and it was his home, such as it was, as well as mine, his hunger as well as my hunger, and if he was sad or sick I had to care, to get involved whether I wanted to or not. There was no longer any way to exist around him, to pretend he was some nameless boy from another country. I had been deeply moved and troubled when the nurse could not arouse Sullivan from that coma. During that drive to Bagnell when I held his limp body against my body, I had cared about him as much or more than I had ever cared about any of my own travails.

But I did not want to play this role. I had myself to look after, and that was enough. I did not want the additional responsibility and worry. I did not want to be big brother, although big brother I was. In name. And that's the way I wanted to keep it. Big brother in name only.

Chapter 14

WHAT IT COMES DOWN TO IS—
THE ONLY PAL YOU'VE REALLY GOT
IS YOURSELF, AND VICE VERSA

After my brother returned the bayonet, Horse Face quieted down. He didn't go so far as to be cooperative, but there was a precipitous drop in his obstreperousness level. As far as I could tell, his relationship with Sullivan was not that of a new-found buddy, but rather Horse Face adopted the role of a belligerent protector. Sullivan was kid stuff for Horse Face, but woe unto anyone who didn't treat Sullivan properly. Horse Face still preferred to do his palling around with his crony, Knuckles, but as far as Sullivan was concerned, starved as he was for a friend, Horse Face filled the bill. It didn't matter that Horse Face's partner in the mess-hall line was Knuckles or that in choosing up for baseball Horse Face selected several bigger kids before he chose Sullivan—what mattered was that he *chose* Sullivan. Also, on one occasion when Knuckles pushed Sullivan against a wall, Horse Face immediately popped Knuckles a good one between his shoulder blades.

I was walking along the trail from Blue Bird Village one afternoon when I heard voices in the adjoining woods and I stopped to investigate. A short distance off the trail I spotted Horse Face and Sullivan sitting with their backs against a tree, sharing a cigarette. Horse Face was obviously an old hand at smoking, but Sullivan was clearly making his debut.

"You ever drink any beer?" Horse Face was saying.

"No—not really."

"You never even *taste* any?"

"Oh, I *tasted* it."

"And?"

"Awful bitter."

"Bitter! Shows what you know! Beer is the most wonderful thing I ever drunk."

"You drink whole glasses?"

"Whole *bottles* is what I drink. Me and my old man. He taught me how you tilt the glass so's it don't foam all over. Sometimes we just sit out on the stoop nights and drink beer and watch everything."

"But don't you get drunk?"

"Naw—it just makes you feel good sittin' there drinkin' beer with your old man."

"I like the *idea* of beer. . . ."

"You ever been in the Budweiser plant and watch 'em mixing the hops and malt and molasses and honey and all the gunk that winds up in beer? That's some sight! And afterwards they give you free drinks."

"I didn't know they put honey in beer."

"Of course they do. That's what gives it the color."

"But then how come it's so bitter?"

"They use bitter honey."

"You sure know a lot of things."

"One thing I know about is beer."

"Now that I know it's got honey, maybe I could get to like it."

"Sure you could—nothin' like sittin' on the stoop with your old man with a good ol' beer and gettin' some drags off his cigarette."

"Don't your mother care?"

"She ain't around."

"Where is she?"

"She works nights at the laundry."

"All night?"

"Yeah—she goes in at six, until six in the A.M. A-course, some nights my old man don't feel good enough to sit outside, so then we don't drink beer." He sat silent for a while, looking up in the trees. "That's most of the time."

"My brother and me both tasted beer oncet and we didn't like it."

"Your brother don't drink beer?"

"No."

"Is he a creep?"

"Who? My brother?"

"Yeah. I can't make up my mind about him."

"You mean 'cause he don't like beer?"

"No, not just that. I mean everything. Like all that Indian shit —painting his face and hopping around and singing in that lousy voice of his."

"I think he's pretty neat."

"Yeah? What about gettin' us down there that night to watch him get eaten by rats? What's neat about that?"

"Was you scared?"

"Are you kidding?"

"Well, everybody else was."

"Anyway, what's so great about scaring a bunch of kids in the dark?"

114

"I thought it was terrific—the pit and the pendulum."

"How'd he do those rats? Did he tell you?"

"I didn't ask him."

"Ask him."

"You don't like him, do you?"

"I ain't made up my mind."

"But you said he was a creeper."

"I say that about a lot of people. That don't mean they maybe ain't all right. Your brother—the thing is he don't like *me*."

"He gave me the bayonet for you."

"Yeah, but he don't like me. That's my trouble. I ain't the kind of person anybody likes."

"I like you, Horse Face."

"No. I just think you want to stay on my good side."

"Listen, Horse Face, I'm your *friend!*"

"I don't know. My old man talks about it a lot. All those pals of his and how when he come back from the war and wasn't, well, okay, how they didn't have time to come around any more. My old man says you look out for yourself—that's the best friend you got."

"If something happened to you, Horse Face, I'd come around to see you. And bring you things."

"What things?"

"Oh, I dunno—things you wanted."

"Look, anything ever happens to me, you bring me some beer. Wherever I am, you smuggle in a couple bottles of cold Griesidieck under your sweater."

"You betcha."

"You'd do that?"

"I sure would."

"Even though you might get caught?"

"No difference."

"Well, I guess we got the last drag outa that." He rubbed out the cigarette butt on the ground. "How'd you like it?"

"It was swell."

"You feel all right? Not sick?"

"No, I feel okay."

"You'll make a good smoker."

Sullivan beamed with pride at this compliment.

"The trouble is that's the only cigarette I got, so you won't be able to practice."

"That's all right—I'll remember."

"That's what I don't like about gettin' stuck in a camp—you ain't got no way to go around and lift a package of cigarettes and a couple of beers."

"It's out of the way, all right."

"I hate to be stuck somewhere where I can't get my hands on things."

I quietly left them in the woods and returned to my cabin. I honestly couldn't tell whether Sullivan had a friend or not.

Chapter 15

A THOUSAND DEATHS, A FELLOW CAN
DIE, IN EVERY BOTTLE OF ROCK 'N RYE

When I got back to my cabin, Babe was there waiting for me. He had organized an evening in Camdenton and he wanted to know if I would like to join in. Since I had never before been invited to participate in Babe's social plans, I figured his invitation was proffered as a token of his regret for the hypnotism debacle.

There were eight of us in Babe's party: Mo and Paul from my village, Bud Fischer, Floyd the cook, Babe, me and two counselors from Blue Bird Village. On the way in, Floyd entertained us with stories about some of the practical jokes he had pulled on various people over the years. Floyd had a wonderful way of making a story come so alive you'd swear it was happening right then and there.

There was this one friend of Floyd's that he told us about whose doctor wanted him to go to the St. Mary's Hospital for some tests, but the man wouldn't go because of a terrible fear he had of hospitals. Finally Floyd talked him into going, but once he was in the hospital, the man was even more nervous and fearful and in a state of near-collapse. Meanwhile, Floyd had arranged for a streetwalker, who was an old friend of his, to dress up in a nun's hospital habit and go into the friend's room soon after he was admitted. The nun-streetwalker began to attend to the friend, straightening up his bed and all that, then she began to caress him and kiss him and finally she got in bed with him.

When Floyd came to visit his friend the following day, he found a changed man, a real hospital *aficionado,* and for the three days of his tests Floyd's friend couldn't have been more cheerful and cooperative, waiting for another visit from the obliging nurse-nun.

When it came time to leave, however, the friend refused to go and it was as difficult to get him to leave the hospital as it had been to get him to enter. Ever since then, Floyd said, his friend had been praying for some affliction that would hospital-ize him again.

Floyd regaled us with stories like that all the way in.

Camdenton was a rather small Ozark town, but there was a CCC camp nearby, and also some of the men who worked on the Bagnell Dam lived in the town. There were two movie houses, three bars, a restaurant, a diner, and a taxi-dance hall called the Club Lido. The first thing we did when we got in was to go to the movies. One movie had *The Duke of West Point,* and the other movie had *Jeepers Creepers.* We decided on *The Duke of West Point;* halfway through it I was sorry we had not chosen *Jeepers Creepers.*

After the movie, we went to the diner for a hamburger and a shake. On our way there, Bud Fischer fainted, but Mo caught him before he fell to the sidewalk. It was a short faint and Mo just held Bud under the arms until he came to. None of the passersby paid much attention to Bud because there were so many CCC men in the town all the time getting drunk.

On our way out of the diner, Floyd suggested that we visit the Club Lido. I knew about taxi-dance halls from that time we lived at the Avalon. There was a taxi-dance in the basement, the Good Times, and there wasn't a night I didn't listen to the band music before I fell asleep, the sour wails of the saxophones coming up the narrow shaft that ran along one side of the building. Taxi-dance music was always slow and rhythmic, music to rub to.

I had actually been in the Good Times only once, when, in desperation, I went down there one night to see if I could get a job. I was only twelve then, hardly an employable age to work behind the bar at a taxi-dance hall, but the owner was quite nice to me. I got a good look at the taxi-dance girls. I thought most of them looked like movie stars in their bright sparkly dresses in the twirling colored lights.

But the girls of the Club Lido were no movie stars. The only ones of our group who actually bought tickets and danced were Floyd and the two Blue Bird counselors. The rest of us stayed at the bar, which was located outside the low railing that demarked the dance area. Babe ordered Griesidieck beer for everyone, but I just let mine sit. As my brother had told Horse Face, I had tried beer once and found it had one of the worst tastes I had ever put in my mouth. Like soap.

Floyd spent five tickets on a pimply blonde with skinny legs who wore a ratty red dress that had a circle of wet where her customers had been rubbing against her all night. I never saw such ratty girls. If someone had given me a free ticket, I wouldn't have used it on any of them. The four men in the band were all drinking, tipping up their glasses while they were playing; it was hard to recognize the tunes they were trying to play.

119

The piano player only played with one hand to keep his drinking hand free. There was a huge fat man who sat at a counter selling tickets. He kept calling over to those of us at the bar, urging us to "get a big dime's worth, come on, boys, your pick of our beauties, here you go, boys, three dances for a quarter." He even sent over one of his "beauties" to hustle us. She had oily hair that was parted in the middle and when she smiled at us I tried not to look at her teeth. She seemed to concentrate on Mo.

"How about it, big boy?" she said, rubbing her hand on the inside of his thigh. "Come over and Polly will show you a go-o-od time!"

"Get lost," Mo said.

She took her hand away like Mo's thigh had suddenly turned to flame. "Go screw yourself," she said.

"It would beat screwing you," Mo said.

Polly went on back to the fat man and said something to him. The fat man turned to look at Mo, and then he turned away and waved his hand at someone toward the back of the dance floor. A big, burly man with some teeth missing materialized out of the tinted darkness.

"We better move it on out of here," Babe said.

I didn't exactly follow what was happening. Babe put some money on the bar for our beers as the burly man started over toward us. As he got closer, I could see that his nose was twisted sideways and there was a heavy scar that ran along the corner of one eye. He was maybe thirty-five, maybe a little more. He walked in a slow way, sort of side to side, and he was looking straight at Mo. He came right up to Mo, very close.

"All right, punk," he said, "what'd you say to the lady?"

I felt a cold streak move up my back.

Mo didn't answer him, but he didn't back down; not an inch.

120

"I'm talkin' to you, punk."

"Look," Babe said placatingly, "I've paid up and we're going, so why don't you—"

"Keep your nose out of this," the bouncer said. "I'm talkin' to this punk here. We don't allow no punks like this to come in here and insult our ladies."

Babe said, "Come on, Mo."

Mo gave the bouncer one last look, then started to follow Babe, but the bouncer was not ready to let him go. He grabbed Mo by the arm in a tight grip. Mo took the bouncer's hand and threw it off his arm.

"You punks are all alike, aren't you?" the bouncer said.

"Stop calling me a punk."

"Aw, listen to that, he don't like to be called a punk. Well, I'll tell you what you really are—a fruit. Nobody but a fruit would come in here and not buy a ticket and bad-mouth one of our dancers. Well, I'm gonna let you in on what we do to fruits. We fix 'em so they don't come back. Not ever. Y'understand?"

He drew back his right arm and threw a heavy punch at Mo's head. Instead of trying to pull away or to duck, Mo lunged forward and as the bouncer's punch landed harmlessly over his shoulder, Mo wrapped his arms around the bouncer's waist in a fierce hug. The bouncer weighed much more than Mo, but Mo had him up off the floor in the circle vise of his arms, slowly increasing the pressure. Mo had his hands locked together behind the bouncer, who strenuously tried to extricate himself but there was nothing he could do. The breath was being squeezed out of him. The bouncer tried to hit Mo with his fists, but, held as he was, all he could do was flail ineffectually at Mo's back. The bouncer's face changed color several times and he made an effort to say something, but all that came out were some gurgling sounds.

The fat ticket-seller, who I guess was the boss, came over to help the bouncer, but Babe and Bud stepped in his way and the ticket-seller didn't go any farther. The bartender was a small, bony man who pretended to be busy washing glasses.

Mo gave one crisp, sudden jerk with his arms and the bouncer passed out. Mo lowered him to the floor beside the bar and we all walked out. It had all happened so quietly and quickly in the dim light of the bar that no one on the dance floor seemed aware of it. But somehow Floyd had seen what was happening. He and the Blue Bird counselors had left and were outside the entrance in the truck with the motor running when we came out. Babe pushed in back of the wheel and we took off.

All the way back we were in a celebratory mood, laughing and recounting what Mo had done to the bouncer. In my fantasies I had often polished off bullies, but this was the first time I had ever seen a real villain get his comeuppance.

When the truck rolled into camp, Babe suggested we all go to his quarters, which were in back of the office. Blanche was in the office, working late, typing reports, so Babe invited her, too.

We crowded into Babe's small room, sitting on the bed and floor. Babe turned on the radio and started to get some things down from his shelf. Olives, sardines, crackers, peanut butter, and a large hunk of dry, granite-hard rat cheese. The last thing he brought out was a bottle that he had hidden in the bottom of his laundry bag. It had ROCK 'N RYE in big letters on its label. With the light behind it, the bottle was beautiful to look at, amber liquid with several white rocks on the bottom, coral in a saffron sea.

I had never tasted liquor, with the exception of that one drink of beer I mentioned previously, primarily because we never had any booze around the house. Not that my parents were teetotalers (I had seen them have a highball when offered one), but because there was never enough money for food, let alone booze. Also, I hated the smell of whiskey. I suppose that dislike stemmed from that time in the Avalon when the room across the hall was occupied, on a regular weekend basis, by a noted criminal lawyer, his blond woman friend, and another man, all of whom stayed in the room, drinking, from Friday afternoon to Sunday night. Their drunken sounds and the pungent smell of the whiskey floated into our room through the open transoms. After that, the very thought of whiskey disgusted me.

But the bottle of Rock 'n Rye which Babe passed around didn't seem like whiskey. Its color, its sweet taste and honey smell resembled Coca-Cola more than booze. Blanche sat down on the floor beside me and began to fix peanut butter and crackers to go with the Rock 'n Rye. It tasted very good. One of the Blue Bird counselors tried to get Blanche's attention, but she seemed to prefer sitting with me. She was a tall girl, about nineteen, who didn't have a very good nose and wore a lot of bright red lipstick. I really didn't like girls with thick lipstick like that, and besides (a) my heart was in Pin Oak, and (b) Blanche had this steady boy friend who came down every Saturday from Sedalia. But I had spent quite a lot of time the past couple of weeks working with Blanche on a camp show for Parents' Day and we had become pretty good friends. Blanche could play the piano and she was able to play the songs I made up for the show. I would write down some lyrics, the way I had composed for our high-school shows, and then sing the words to some melody I invented. Blanche was able to listen to me sing the song and then right away play it on the piano. I had always been in awe of piano players. A couple of times Blanche pointed out how one of my new songs closely resembled some well-known tune, whereupon I would toss it away and make up another song.

The radio was tuned to a station in nearby Eldon that was bringing the music of Ben Bernie and his lads from the College Inn in Chicago. Blanche was a quiet, rather shy type who never talked much when we were working on the show, but as the Rock 'n Rye made its rounds, sipping it and nibbling the peanut-butter crackers, she began talking a blue streak. How much she liked my songs, and what fun she had when we got together. On and on. And about some uncle of hers who was with Tin Pan Alley in New York City and how she planned to send him some of my stuff to see if he would publish it.

Blanche began to sing along with Ben Bernie, who was singing, if you could call it that, "I'm in the Mood for Love." As Blanche was singing I found my eyes riveted on her lips, all that moving lipstick, and I began to giggle.

"I feel like dancing," Blanche said, putting her arm around mine.

"There's no room," I said.

She sat there holding my arm and humming along with Ben Bernie. "Oh, let's dance," she said, squeezing my arm against her breast. I was watching her moving lipstick and giggling.

"I know," she said. "Let's go across to my room. We can dance to my radio." She had a room in back of the other side of the office. She stood up, holding on to my arm, and pulled me to my feet.

"Where you two going?" Babe asked.

"We'll be right back," Blanche said.

They all made derisive noises of disbelief as we left the room. Their voices sounded far away, coming from the distant end of a tunnel.

When we entered Blanche's room she immediately turned on the radio. Instead of Ben Bernie there was a woman singing,

> When did you leave heaven,
> How could they let you go?
> How's everything in heaven?
> I'd like to know,
> Yes, I'd like to kno-ow. . . .

Blanche put her body against mine and started to dance, singing in my ear. She moved her body against mine in rhythm to the music, her breasts moving from side to side while her hips moved up and down. She was certainly well coordinated. I had never before danced like that. If the Club Lido girls charged a dime, Blanche was definitely worth two bits.

"You excite me," she said and she moved her lips from my ear onto my mouth. I could feel the thick lipstick smearing off on me. It tasted like cherries. Blanche was getting very excited, but as she started to kiss me, I began to feel rather sick, a heavy, lumpish feeling in my stomach. I also felt a little guilty about being unfaithful to Connie. But what I mostly felt was that lump in my stomach.

"Listen, lock the door," she said.

My face felt hot and my forehead was quite damp. She turned out the light. I could hear her moving around in the dark.

"I'm over here," she said.

I followed her voice. She was in bed. She pulled me down beside her and put her lips on mine. She still had plenty of lipstick. My hand touched her back and to my surprise she had taken off her clothes. I had never been with a naked girl before, and certainly never been in bed with one. I touched around on her to be sure she was naked all over. She was. I should have been out of my head with excitement, for here was the moment

I had so often thought about and fantasized, but my head felt funny now and the lump had moved up from my stomach to my chest. Blanche began to unbutton my shirt. Her breasts felt wonderfully soft and warm against my chest. She was terribly excited.

"Oh, oh," she said. "Please hurry, hurry and take me."

I started to unbutton my pants. The lump was in my throat now and my head was pounding. My mouth was flannel dry. Sweat was pouring off my forehead and running down the side of my face.

"Blanche, look . . . Blanche . . ."

She was holding me for dear life and moaning and urging me to hurry. I was struggling to break her grip on me while trying to keep the lump down in my throat. My whole body was pouring sweat. I gave a mighty heave and rolled out of her grasp. I grabbed my shirt and headed for the door, bumping into everything in the room on my way.

"Where you going? Are you crazy?" Blanche was hissing at me. "How can you leave me like this? You bastard! Come back, oh, please come back."

I just made it through the door when the lump surged loose and I threw up. I'd never thrown up like that before. It seemed to come up from my socks, and my body heaved in great spasms. It came up through my nose. I had trouble breathing. I was terribly scared. I couldn't catch my breath between vomits. I wished to God my mother had been there. Somehow I managed to stagger over to the infirmary building, which was not far from the office. Although a dim light was burning, the room was deserted. In the middle of a table at the door was a sign: RING FOR EMERGENCY. I pushed the button; immediately I had to go outside to throw up again.

Miss Collins came into the infirmary, tying up her bathrobe.

At first she didn't see me retching outside the door, but then she heard me. She gave me something white to drink, but I continued to vomit. She kept asking me what had I eaten, where did it hurt, but I was too sick to answer. I had never been so sick in my whole life. Miss Collins dug her fingers into my stomach to see if I had appendicitis. She studied my tongue. She probed for tender places in my abdomen. Through it all, I vomited.

From the shelf Miss Collins took down a large bottle labeled IPECAC and filled a shot glass with its contents.

"Drink it down," she commanded.

It looked awful. I shook my head. I wanted to ask her to phone my mother, but we didn't have a phone. Miss Collins put her left hand under my head and pushed it up while with her right hand she stuck the ipecac under my nose.

"Drink!" she bellowed. She started to tilt the glass, so it was either take it down the throat or up the nose. It was the foulest stuff I had ever had in my mouth. I howled.

"Shut up!" she commanded.

"Oh, God," I moaned.

"If you can keep that down you'll be all right."

I threw it up. She put another dose down me.

"I wish I had a stomach pump," she said. She asked me again and again if I had eaten anything or drunk anything, but I only moaned and groaned.

After the second dose of ipecac, I didn't throw up any more, but I continued to gasp for air and exude sweat from every pore. Miss Collins gave me a pill that she said would make me sleep.

"I don't want to sleep," I said. "I want to die."

She bathed my face with a cold washcloth and after a while I passed out.

Sullivan was sitting beside my bed when I awoke. Hot sun rays slanted onto the sheet that covered me, but I had stopped sweating. Sullivan's close face was anxiously peering into mine. I felt like my insides had turned to plaster of Paris.

Sullivan shook my arm. "Wake up," he said. "Are you waked up?"

I grunted.

"How do you feel?"

"Like death," I mumbled.

Sullivan moved his face even closer, to get my ultimate attention. "No, listen, A, no dying, you hear? I'm counting on you . . . not to die." There were tears in the bottom of his eyes. I realized, looking at myself through Sullivan's eyes, what I currently represented in his uncertain world.

"Oh, I don't mean *really* die," I said, my vomit-sore stomach hurting with every syllable I spoke.

"Well, what do you mean?"

"Nothing. Just that I feel lousy. But I'll be all right."

"Promise?"

"Promise. Cross my heart and hope to die."

"There you go again."

"That's an expression."

"Just don't say die, all right?"

"All right."

"What was it, ptomaine?"

"Something like that."

"Well, you got to get better—it's my birthday tomorrow, remember?"

"Oh, sure." I hadn't remembered.

"You think Floyd will remember?"

"You bet. You're going to have the best camp birthday of all."

"A—listen, I was awful scared this morning." Only my mother and Sullivan called me A.

"Why?"

"When they came and said you were in the hospital. Some-body said you'd been poisoned."

"I'm okay."

"When I heard them say poison I thought maybe you'd croaked."

"Not me."

"And, you see, you're practically the only one who cares about me."

"What about Mother and—"

"Uh-uh. Nobody cares about you who sends you off to Keo-kuk."

"But we had to live in that lousy one room."

"They didn't send *you* away, did they?"

"I was bigger."

"But I was littler, so I took up less room and ate less."

"Now, Sullivan, Mother cares about you and you know it."

"Yes, but she don't care like you do."

"How can you tell I care?"

"You *do,* that's all. Like this birthday. You care that I have a big cake and all. Mother and Dad never—aw, you know about birthdays."

"Don't be too hard on them, Sullivan. They do their best."

"Oh, sure, listen, I 'preciate them. But I'd 'preciate them more if they . . ." He suddenly didn't want to talk about it any more. That was the way with Sullivan—he could only feel sorry for himself to a point, then he seemed to realize it was best to drop it and veer off into positive things. "But I'm glad you're not dead, hey! Can I do something for you? You need anything?"

"No. I'll be all right by this afternoon."

"You better be—I'm cutting you the biggest piece of my cake. You remember what I want wrote on it?"

I assured him that I did.

"You want to really know why I want a cake so much?"

"Yes, why do you?"

"Because I've got so many important wishes to make." With that he ran off so as not to be late for his beloved wrestling session.

I had indeed forgotten about Sullivan's all-important birthday. After he left, I gingerly sat up, tested my head and my stomach, and tentatively tried to stand up. My head felt disconnected, but I forced myself to get dressed and go to the dining hall. I thought about that bottle of Rock 'n Rye and I felt like throwing up again. Also, my misery induced despairing thoughts, never far from my surface, about having to pass up college in the fall.

Floyd was busy at the stove. The food odors emanating from the kitchen almost forced me to turn back.

"Hello, hello," Floyd said. "You look terrible."

"Oh, I'm fine," I said. I didn't want him to know what Rock 'n Rye had done to me.

"You look like yesterday's scrambled eggs."

"Listen, Floyd, have you gotten a notice from the office that it's my brother's birthday tomorrow?"

He looked at some slips that were pinned to a chopping block with an ice pick.

"Yeah, here we are—Sullivan."

"Well, do me a favor, will you? It's a big birthday for him, so will you make a special cake and write A MILLION HAPPY BIRTH-DAYS on it? Here, I've written it down."

Floyd told me to leave it to him.

On my way out of the dining hall I ran into Blanche, who looked right at me but didn't say hello or anything.

Chapter 16

THE SUN BROKE THROUGH AND THE
ANGEL FLEW IN FROM WATERMAN AVENUE

I trudged back to my cabin from the mess hall on legs made
of old spaghetti. My head throbbed worse than ever. Life was
as bleak as it had ever been. I could barely make it to my cot.

As I tenderly lowered my head I felt something on the pillow
—it was a letter that my blurry eyes had not seen. I looked at
the return address: The Scholarship Foundation of St. Louis.
That reminded me of my dismal fate in the fall and I felt even
worse.

I opened the letter:

> Dear Aaron:
>
> I am really terribly pleased to inform you of one of those
> rare scholarship miracles that has befallen you.
>
> As I told you, all of our scholarship money was allotted
> for the coming academic year, but last week a philanthro-
> pist who normally contributes to our funding, but who had
> been out of the country for the past year, returned to St.
> Louis and gave us a substantial contribution.

I convened the Committee for the express purpose of seeing if they wished to authorize a special scholarship for you out of this unexpected windfall. I'm happy to tell you that, having met you at my bridge party, they were unanimously in favor of granting you such aid. This means you will have a full scholarship for the entire school year 1936–1937.

When you return from camp, please come to see me so that we can execute the necessary papers. I must frankly say that it is moments like these that make all our arduous work worthwhile. I thought about you and your sad plight many times after your visit, and I don't know when any good turn of events has made me happier.

> With all our good wishes,
> Sincerely,
> Mrs. I. Bettman.

I started to cry. Just like that. I covered my face with the letter and let myself cry. Nothing better had ever happened to me, and it couldn't have come at a better time. A stranger, a woman I had seen once, barged in on, imposed myself on—for her to care so much, to give me such an enormous gift. The gift of being myself, of feeling equal; the light-hearted joy of looking forward; of feeling that someday I would be everything I had felt I could be.

All this from a stranger.

Chapter 17

WHY PUT A ROSE ON THE GRAVE
IF THE CORPSE CAN'T SMELL IT?

I was on the top of a ladder helping to hang an INDIAN MOUND sign over the entrance to our village, the letters made of branches, when a runner arrived summoning me to Big Chief Berman's office.

"You have a camper you call Horse Face."

"It's a name that came with him."

"Well, I just got a call—his father died. Have him pack all his things and the truck will take him to the bus in Jefferson City."

"I don't think he has any money."

"We'll get his bus ticket and give him carfare for when he gets to St. Louis."

Horse Face was in back of his cabin, throwing a knife into a tree trunk at ten paces—he was very good at it.

"That's pretty good, Horse Face."

"Okay—you came to crab about me not bein' at woodcraft, right?"

"No."

"Well, I'm sick o' that goddam totem pole. That's all we do is sandpaper that goddam totem pole."

"Listen, Horse Face, sit down here a minute—I want to talk to you."

He eyed me suspiciously, but sat down beside me.

"We've had our little differences, you and me, but I want you to know you've improved a hell of a lot."

"Maybe it's you who's improved."

"Maybe. I never thought of it that way."

"You were pretty pukey."

"Anyway, I just wanted to talk to you."

"I shouldn'ta skipped that goddam totem pole, I know, but I woked up this morning feelin' bad."

"In what way?"

"I woked up thinkin' about my old man and feelin' bad."

"What were you thinking?"

"Oh, I dunno—I just had a bad feelin' about him. You see, there's nobody to look after him when I'm away."

"I thought your mother and your Aunt Bernice—"

"Oh, yeah, but it's not the same for my old man as when it's me. A-course, sometimes when his head is funny he don't much know who I am, but then sometimes he knows all about me and we play casino and listen to the ballgames. I'm a Cardinal fan and he's strictly for the Browns, but it don't matter—I listen to his and he listens to mine. He likes to chew tobacco during the games. Other times too. He says it soothes him. But usually he ain't got none 'cause we ain't got the money to buy it. So when he runs out and really wants some I go out and lift it. I used to have to go into cigar stores and snatch it and run, and once I almost got caught—got knocked down and just barely got away

—but now I figured out how to get into Christmeyer's tobacco shop at night and I only take a couple at a time and they ain't wised up yet."

"Horse Face, I really came to find you because I have something to tell you about him."

"My old man?"

"Yes."

"Something bad?"

"You know how sick he's been—how he suffers . . ."

"He's dead, ain't he?"

"Yes. That's what I came to tell you."

"Oh, hell—and I wasn't there."

"I'm sure he was glad you were in camp."

"When I told him goodbye, it was one of his days he didn't know who I was."

"What you want to do now is remember all the good times you had . . ."

"Sure, that's all he had—good times. What the hell you talkin' about, rememberin' good times?"

"But you said the ballgames—"

"You ever seen anybody'd been gassed? We'd be sittin' there, everything nice, and alla sudden he'd turn crazy—punchin' me and hollerin' and wettin' his pants, the spit comin' out of his mouth, hollerin' crazy sounds and knockin' over the furniture. Then when it was over, he'd . . . he'd cry. . . ." Horse Face started to cry. "He'd sit down on the floor and cry like he was three years old."

I put my arm around Horse Face's skinny shoulders. He bowed his head, his tears dropping onto the ground.

"I wish I coulda seen him like he was before—just once. My ma says he was the strongest man she ever knew." He turned his face to look at me, the tears running along his pointed nose. "What am I gonna do now? I really liked my old man."

"You're going to take his place. That's how it works—the fathers die and the sons grow up strong and fresh to take their place. You're going to be someone he'd be proud of."

"Crap. I'm gonna be another punk outa Dago Hill."

"When I get back to St. Louis, I'll be glad to see you, Horse Face. Sullivan, too."

"I won't be around."

"Where you going?"

"I dunno—somewheres."

"How about your mother?"

"She don't like me."

"Now, come on . . ."

"Most of the time, she don't even talk to me."

"Well, *now* she will. Things will be different."

"You don't know my old lady."

"Promise me you'll wait till I get back to St. Louis."

"No, I'll go back and bury my old man and take off."

"It'll be tough for a kid your age to get along. You should stay in school."

"Yeah. Sure. My old man stayed in school—he was a high-school graduate—and look where it got him."

"But he had the bad luck of the war."

"Well, it's always somethin'. I ain't waitin' around for *my* bad luck."

Horse Face had stopped crying. He eased away from my arm and stood up. "How do I get back to St. Louis?"

"We're putting you on the Jefferson City bus."

"I better pack."

"You want help?"

"No."

"Your father would want you to stay put and go to school and make something of yourself."

"My father is dead. He don't want nothin'."

Chapter 18

A MILLION HAPPY BIRTHDAYS,
COUNT 'EM—BUT DON'T COUNT THIS ONE

The dining hall was one vast rectangular room with screen on three sides. All of Camp Hiawatha ate at the same time, Indian Mound occupying four tables in the center of the hall.

Sullivan was so excited over the advent of his birthday festivities that he spent the whole meal alternately watching Big Chief Berman and the kitchen door, not touching his food. He knew that he was the only kid in camp with a birthday that day, which meant that he would have undivided attention. On our way into the dining room he had immediately checked to be sure that Big Chief Berman had a present beside his chair. I had already given Sullivan my presents, a bow and six arrows that Corny Barmowitz had made for me in his woodworking shop, and a pocket knife I had bought for thirty-five cents from Bud Fischer.

As the meal ended, Chief Berman tapped a knife against his water glass and stood up. "May I have your attention, please?" he said. "We have a birthday boy today, Sullivan Hotchner of Indian Mound Village, and it's number eleven for him."

There was a scatter of applause and a few whistles. Sullivan blushed.

"Congratulations, Sullivan, and here's a little something from all of us."

The Chief picked up the present and proffered it to Sullivan, who went over very self-consciously to receive it. He said thank you to the Chief and unwrapped the present, which was an American flag.

As soon as Sullivan got back to his seat, the kitchen door opened and in came Floyd carrying a huge birthday cake with eleven candles on it and a giant sparkler crackling in the center. It was three times bigger than any of the previous birthday cakes. Ornately covered with red and white icing, it had spun-sugar roses in bas-relief all along its perimeter. Floyd had certainly lived up to his promise. Sullivan's hands shot up to his cheeks as he jumped up from his seat. A pervasive *ooh!* and *wow!* swept the dining hall, and the campers gave the cake a much bigger hand than they had given Sullivan.

As Floyd put the cake in front of Sullivan, the sparkler anointing him with its flying sparks, everyone began to sing "Happy Birthday." Sullivan looked at his beautiful cake with its inscribed A MILLION HAPPY BIRTHDAYS FOR SULLIVAN, the birthday music filling his ears, and a smile of pure, unadulterated happiness came over his face. He stood over the cake, which was the size of a lady's hatbox and came up to his chin, closed his eyes, and made his wishes. Then he opened his eyes, took a couple of practice breaths, and with one giant effort blew out the twelve candles. The hot stem of the spent sparkler continued to glow. The campers gave Sullivan a nice hand.

Floyd handed Sullivan a large knife to cut the cake, and held a plate at the ready to receive the first piece. Sullivan carefully placed the knife so that the point was at dead center, then pushed down on it, but the knife did not make the cut. Now Sullivan put both hands on the handle and bore down hard, but he didn't make a dent in the cake. He picked up the blade and looked at it.

"I musta forgot to sharpen it," Floyd said.

Some of the campers, impatient to get at the cake, began to make fun of Sullivan for his lack of muscle. A third try also failed.

"Try cutting from the edge," Floyd suggested.

Sullivan put the blade against the edge of the cake and vigorously cut back and forth with it several times, but the knife stayed right on the surface. The campers were beginning to laugh and hoot now. I couldn't imagine why Sullivan could not cut his cake, no matter how dull the knife. Sullivan tried again and again, every which way, beginning to lose his temper, getting red in the face from his efforts.

I was just about to go over and help him, when Sullivan took the knife and scraped away some of the icing. Then he banged the blade against the heavy cardboard underneath. The room exploded with laughter at the cardboard cake, all the boys crowding forward to get a glimpse of Floyd's latest practical joke.

Through the tangle of the campers, I caught sight of Sullivan. There was a stricken look on his face and tears were running down his cheeks. The laughter was deafening. Sullivan threw down the knife and ran from the room.

"Wait, stop him!" Floyd yelled. "I got the real cake . . ."

But Sullivan was gone.

Floyd came over to me. "Go get him," he said. "I've got a real cake for him. This was just a joke. Can't he take a joke?"

"No," I said, "he can't."

I took my time walking back to Indian Mound. I wanted to give Sullivan a little time to compose himself. I really wasn't mad at Floyd—how could he know what that cake meant to Sullivan? I tried desperately to think of something that I could say to Sullivan. He had again been betrayed, and I was party to it, albeit unwittingly.

I went to Sullivan's cabin and peered through the screen. He wasn't there. I went to my cabin, the rec hall, the waterfront, but he was nowhere I looked. I told one of the boys in Sullivan's cabin to alert me the minute he showed up, then I went back to my cabin to wait for him. Probably went for a walk, I thought.

That time of the year the Ozarks began to get dark around seven thirty. By eight o'clock, when there still was no sign of Sullivan, I began to worry. I went up to the office and told Babe about him. He sent runners to the other villages in our camp, to find out if they had seen Sullivan or knew of his whereabouts. Word came back that he hadn't been seen.

At nine o'clock Babe and I went to see Chief Berman. The Chief became angry because we had not come to him sooner.

"Where do you think he would go?" Berman asked me.

"I don't know. He was so hurt and angry he might have gone anywhere."

"But where? Would he be more likely to follow a road or go plunging into the woods?"

"I don't know, but I'm going out to look for him."

"We're *all* going out, but we have to be coordinated."

"Do you think he'd do anything that involved the lake?" Babe asked. "Like taking a boat?"

"No," I said, "he just barely knows how to swim."

"Do you have a photograph of him?" the Chief asked.

"No."

"Well, let's wait an hour or so, and if he's not back by then I'll call the police."

In the next hour, Mo, Paul, and I went through the entire

141

camp, but there was no sign of Sullivan. From the moment he left the dining hall, no one had laid eyes on him.

After Big Chief Berman alerted the state police, he organized two search parties, one to go north of the camp, the other to go south. I went with Babe's group, which headed south. We worked our way slowly over the dense terrain, using flashlights, calling, whistling, covering all but the totally impenetrable areas. But the region was so vast that by morning we had not gone very far.

We returned to Camp Hiawatha, covered with mosquito welts, hoping for good news from Chief Berman's contingent, but they had had no better luck. The police came with hound dogs, which sniffed Sullivan's clothes to establish a scent. All the local radio stations were called and given a bulletin with Sullivan's description, to broadcast every hour. Local police within a fifty-mile radius were alerted.

After breakfast, our group went back to continue the search; we worked all day long, but by five o'clock there was still no sign of Sullivan. All I felt was a kind of drained numbness. All night and day I had called his name and sounded my shrill two-fingered whistle that he would have recognized if he had heard it. It was stifling, humid hot as only the Ozarks can get. I had a sudden feeling that Sullivan was dead. A night in this thick undergrowth with all its perils, its mosquitoes and copperheads ... I dropped in my tracks and leaned my back against the trunk of an old tree. Far off I could hear the hound dogs searching. I closed my eyes and tried to blot out the premonition that Sullivan was dead. I couldn't.

The other members of my group had probably moved on without me, not noticing that I had dropped out. A small plane flew low overhead, perhaps part of the search. I was too tired to think clearly about what had happened and what was happening. The event in the dining room had occurred with the swiftness of a street accident. Now, sitting there in the suffocating heat of the late afternoon, I tried to think of what I could have done or should have done while Sullivan was being made the butt of Floyd's crude joke. Even with hindsight's help, I could not think of anything. But what bothered me most was that I had done *nothing,* just sat there doing *nothing,* and certainly I could have done *something.* If only I had taken the knife from Sullivan and tried to cut the cake myself, then the joke would have been on *me.*

Where could Sullivan have gone? Oh, where? I could not hear the dogs any more. I felt utterly defeated. As I leaned my head against the tree and thought about Sullivan, what I remembered was the time we lived on Art Hill Place, just before the Depression. It was a nice apartment at the top of a steep hill overlooking Forest Park. My mother and father were both working then, and we had paid help to take care of us. There was this one girl, Thelma, who came to the apartment one day with a man who explained about her to my mother. The man was the placement counselor at a home for unwed mothers, and this girl, who had just become a mother, was living at the home with her baby. The home placed the girls in domestic jobs to help pay for their upkeep.

My mother hired Thelma, who was sixteen years old and very pretty. I was nine at the time and I remember asking my mother why Thelma always had two circles of wet on the front of her dress where her breasts were. My mother explained that that was milk for her new baby.

One of Thelma's duties was to take us to Forest Park to play. To get to the park, it was necessary to cross a wide expanse of streetcar tracks that ran along the bottom of Art Hill, parallel to the park. My mother had laid down a hard and fast rule that

143

Sullivan and I were *never* to cross those tracks by ourselves. There had once been a serious accident there, and my mother, who was by nature a fearful woman, made us promise that we'd never, ever go across those tracks unless we were with a grownup.

One afternoon, a few days after Thelma had started work, she took us across the tracks into the park where there was a play area. After a little while she told me to look after Sullivan for a few minutes, that she'd be right back. For a while I played ball with some kids my age while Sullivan played tag, then he and I walked around looking at things. I spotted a couple of birds' nests and right away Sullivan had one of the great schemes he was always proposing. "Listen," he said excitedly, "why don't we get a lot of bird nestes and put them all together in one tree with nails and a hammer and then they can all live together and be happy and eat clams like eagles do." For a four-year-old, he certainly had grandiose schemes.

It was early afternoon when Thelma left, but by four thirty she had not returned. Sullivan and I stood at the park side of the tracks, looking for her, but she wasn't around.

I looked up and down the tracks. There was nothing coming. "Come on," I said, "give me your hand."

"No," Sullivan said, putting his hand behind him.

"Look—there's nothing coming."

"No. Mom said no."

"But that dumb, stupid Thelma dumped us here!"

"I wait."

Far away we could see a streetcar coming.

"What if she never comes back," I said, "you gonna spend your whole doggone life here?"

"Looka that streetcar," Sullivan said. "It could squish your guts all over."

144

"Okay, look, after it passes, we cross, okay?"

The streetcar went by with a rackety clatter, sending dust and sparks off the track.

"Now, come on," I said, "give me your hand."

"No."

"Then I'm going without you."

"I'll tell Mom."

"Go ahead. See if I care."

"I will."

"Come *on*, Sullivan!"

"No."

"I'll leave you—I mean it."

"No, no, no!"

I ran across the tracks, leaving Sullivan standing there. Across the tracks there was a row of stores—a cleaner's, a grocery store, a Greek luncheonette, a bar. As I passed the bar, I saw Thelma sitting there with a man. She was drinking and smoking a cigarette. At first I thought I'd yell in at her, but I didn't. I ran all the way up the hill to our apartment. It was after five by now and my mother was home.

"What! You left your brother there by himself? Next to those tracks?"

"He wouldn't come."

"That's a terrible, terrible thing to do!"

"What about Thelma? Don't get mad at *me!*"

We were hurrying down the hill.

"Never mind about Thelma. She'll get hers."

"Leaving two little boys like that," I said.

"I told you never to cross those tracks."

"But we were stuck there."

"I don't care—what if something happened to Sullivan?"

"Oh, he's all right. You'll see."

Sullivan was precisely where I had left him. My mother went across the tracks and picked him up. Then we all three went to the bar. My mother stood in the open door and called Thelma, who came out on the sidewalk.

My mother was in a rage. "How could you leave these little boys? I told you about the tracks!"

"I was just on my way back to get them," Thelma said.

"You tramp," my mother said. "Here you are full of baby's milk and you're picking up men at bars. Your kind should never be given a decent chance. I pity that baby of yours. Now, get up there and pack up your things."

"Who needs your stinkin' job? You and your stinkin' kids."

"You're not a nice lady," Sullivan said.

Thinking about Sullivan, who was four at the time, standing there on the other side of the tracks, sticking to the rules, patiently waiting, I felt a surge of hope that perhaps he wasn't dead. What was in his favor was that by nature he was a survivor. The Art Hill tracks. Keokuk. The ghastly ear abscesses. So maybe, wherever he was, he would survive this.

Chapter 19

IF YOU *FEEL* LOVE, EVEN THOUGH
YOU DON'T *SAY* LOVE, IS THAT ENOUGH?

As I suspected, I had lost contact with Babe's group, so I continued to search on my own. The dense woods I had been searching suddenly broke into a clearing beyond which there was a small town. All of the houses were on two streets, so it was easy to go from house to house, asking whoever answered if they had seen a small boy of Sullivan's description.

No one had. But when I went into the grocery store, the storekeeper told me that a boy who fitted that description had come into the store that morning to buy some crackers.

"Did he come from around here?"

"Nope—is why I mention him. Never seen him afore."

"Maybe I should ask the police."

"No police here. But up the road a piece in Harmonyville there's a sheriff."

I tried to hitch a ride, but only two cars and a truck went by and none stopped.

Harmonyville consisted of one street with houses and three

stores. I asked someone where I'd find the sheriff and he directed me to the barber shop.

There was a man in the chair getting a haircut and a boy reading a Little Orphan Annie comic book. I asked the barber if he knew where I could find the sheriff. He looked up at me over his scissors.

"You're speakin' to him," he said.

"Oh, sir, I'm looking for my eleven-year-old brother who ran away from camp. I was told there was a boy around about here today who might be him. I thought maybe you might know something about him, this boy who was seen around here today."

"Yep. There he is." He pointed with his scissors at the boy with the comic book. "He run away from Eldenton. Waitin' for his pa to come git him." The sheriff went back to work on his customer. "Lot o' boys runnin' away this time o' year."

I went on out of the barber shop, bitterly disappointed. I had really thought, from the grocery man's description, that the boy he had seen was Sullivan. The rise and fall of my hopes had left me feeling more hopeless than before.

I walked along the dirt road of the town. The evening light was getting darker. I was very tired, too tired to care about eating. I kept turning Art Hill Place and the car tracks over and over in my mind. I couldn't stop thinking about it. Sullivan at the tracks. Thelma. Art Hill Place, the last decent home we had had, the place we lived the longest during all those migratory years, going from one flat (in St. Louis an apartment for which you had to furnish your own heat was called a flat) to another, a jump ahead of the foreclosing landlord, getting a few months' concession (pay one month's rent, get three months free before the lease began to run) and then sneaking out at the end of the concession.

148

Well, I'd have to face it: my mother had to be told. Berman had asked for her phone number, but I had stalled him by saying we didn't have a phone—which was true. But we lived above Sorkin's delicatessen, and although Sorkin wasn't crazy about our getting calls there, it was possible to reach my mother on Sorkin's phone. If Sullivan didn't appear by morning, I'd have to telephone her. God, how I dreaded that. My mother had gone through enough—the depredations of the Depression, her confinement in the Fee-Fee Sanitorium for consumption, my father's heart attack, and now . . . this. I felt terribly guilty about Sullivan's disappearance, for not having protected him, almost as if I myself had played the cake joke on him.

I had no idea how far I was from Camp Hiawatha. It was getting quite dark. I went into the general store. It didn't smell very good. More cat piss than soap and coffee. I asked the old lady behind the counter if there was a phone that I could use for an emergency call. She took me through a door back of the store where she lived.

The operator put the call right through. Babe answered the phone. He was very glad to hear from me. "I thought we'd lost both of you," he said.

I asked about Sullivan. No sign of him, Babe said. The police had followed several leads, but none led to Sullivan. Chief Berman had again asked how he could reach my mother. I said I would try to call her myself in the morning.

I paid the old woman for the phone, and bought a bag of pretzels, a pint bottle of milk, and an apple, for seven cents. Afterward I walked along the dirt highway until I found a field with a haystack. I got comfortable in the hay and started to eat my dinner, but I fell asleep before I could finish it.

I woke in the night feeling chilly and full of a dream about Sullivan that I tried to remember, but it was just beyond me. I dug deeper into the haystack for warmth. There were nearby animal noises, but the full moon's brilliant light counteracted them. I ate a few pretzels and fell asleep again.

When I next woke, the sun was up and the field dripped dew. I had been dreaming again, this time about the streetcar tracks; as I struggled to recollect the dream, I unexpectedly recalled something about Art Hill, something that startled me into sitting up abruptly; as the remembrance sharpened, I came fully to life. I jumped up, dusted the hay off me, and ran to the road. At that early hour, the sun just up, there wasn't much traffic, but the first truck that came along, a rickety Ford with some crates of chickens, I stepped out in the road and waved my arms. No time to be reticent about hitchhiking.

The driver was grumpy about having to stop, but he gave me a lift anyway. The chickens made a lot of noise and they smelled pretty bad.

The farmer dropped me off where the spur road to Camp Hiawatha transected the highway. I ran all the way to the camp. Of course, I could again be chasing a false lead, but not if I was right about connecting what had happened that time we moved from Art Hill to what had happened now.

The camp was not awake yet, so I encountered no one as I ran along the path that led to Indian Mound. I stopped for a moment in front of the rec hall, then ran around to the rear. There was a ladder lying on the ground. I propped it up against the building and began to climb up to the roof.

The moving van had been packed and ready to go when my mother discovered that Sullivan was missing. That's what I had suddenly recalled, that incident at Art Hill Place when we couldn't find Sullivan. I went up and down the block and my mother and father canvassed the neighbors, but Sullivan was nowhere to be found. Three or four hours of searching, my mother's anxiety mounting, and then Mrs. Harmon on the third floor came out to say that she'd thought she saw Sullivan going up to the roof.

I stepped off the ladder and onto the roof of the rec hall. There were two large galvanized ventilators at one end and a broad brick chimney at the other. I walked across the roof to the chimney, hoping against hope. At first look he wasn't there, and my heart dropped, but I walked around to the other side of the chimney and there, in the sheltered, hidden space between the buttress of the building and the chimney, was Sullivan. He sat with his back against the chimney, sound asleep. Beside him was the American flag he had received from Chief Berman.

As I sat down beside him, he awoke.

"Hi," I said. "How are you?"

He didn't answer. He bent his head forward and looked down at the roof between his legs.

"You must be hungry," I said. I still had a couple of pretzels in my pocket and I offered him one. Sullivan looked at it and hesitated before he took it. He took a bite, but he didn't eat hungrily.

"Can I go home?" he asked. "I don't want to stay here any more."

"Sure, if you want to. But what's there to do at home?"

"I just want to go home."

Home, those three rooms over Sorkin's delicatessen. Sullivan slowly munched his pretzel. We just sat there for a while, saying nothing.

"About the cake," he finally said, "does it mean I don't get my wishes?"

"Sure you do. You blew out all the candles, didn't you?"

"Yes, but you don't get wishes off a phony cake."

"Oh, I don't know about that."

I turned to look at him. He was so skinny and vulnerable. I had never told anyone that I loved them. Not my mother, not anyone. I loved her, all right, but I could never get the words out. Maybe it was a question of courage.

But now, feeling as I did about Sullivan, I felt I could tell him that I loved him; I felt I could actually say the words. I doubt that anyone had ever said that to him. Our family just didn't say that to one another. I put my hand on his arm and he turned his head sideways to look up at me.

"Sullivan, listen," I said; I really had it in my mouth to tell him that I loved him; the words were there, and I tried to say them, but I couldn't. I looked at him and I *felt* the love I had for him, but that's as far as it went.

He studied my faltering lips and worried face, and he managed a faint smile. I think at that moment he knew I loved him. He must have felt it. Certainly he knew that I cared, that I was not just his brother, but also his friend.

Sullivan picked up his flag, got up, and started to walk toward the ladder. So did I.